Blood Curse

PULSE Vampire Series Book 8

kailin gow

1

Blood Curse (Pulse #8)

Blood Curse (PULSE Vampire Series Book 8)

Published by Sparklesoup Inc.
Copyright © 2013 Kailin Gow

For information, please contact:
Sparklesoup.com
Second Edition.
Printed in the United States of America.

DEDICATION

This book series is dedicated to all the nameless volunteer blood donors, my doctor, and nurses at Las Colinas Medical Center in Texas who helped me pull through when I had suffered extreme blood loss, blacked out, and nearly hit my head on the floor. Your team gave me bags of blood for transfusion, which helped restore me to a level of safety.My body craved the blood to keep alive, yet the thought of having to receive the blood from others because my own body couldn't generate it fast enough, made me empathize with vampires like Jaegar and Stuart.

When faced with death by blood loss, you realize how precious that blood in your veins and that beat in your heart are. Thank you blood donors around the world for providing this pulse for me and everyone who may at one point or another require your gift.

Sincerely,

Kailin

Prologue

Scorched. The sands burned with the heat of the blazing sun that would have scorched the feet of mortal men, leaving angry red marks across the soles of their shoes. The air was dry, so dry that mortal men would have coughed it up, spluttered up blood as the sands corrugated the insides of their throats. This was no place for mortal men, this desert in the middle of nowhere, these Saharan breezes that whipped the cheek with grains of sand as hard as diamonds, these lacerating winds so full of emptiness, of death. But that did not matter to Samson. He had not been a mortal man for centuries.

Days, years, centuries had gone by since a desert like this would have frightened him. He had seen much, known much, since then. He had said goodbye to all his mortal woes, mortal fears, to everything that he had known of the past. It wasn't difficult for him, after all. His human life had hardly been anything to brag about. It had been misery, unending misery. And sand.

Samson had been a gladiator, after all, in the days of Ancient Rome. He had been one of the gladiators who had fought in the Coliseum. He had been a killer, hardened and trained, from the moment one of the commanders at the gladiatorial training school picked him up by the scruff of the neck, whelping young lad that he was, crying and mewing, and told him that he had two choices. "Kill or die." It was that simple. He fought for the entertainment of the roaring crowds, the *bread and circuses*, they said, the entertainment of those who did not have to worry about performing to the crowd while dodging a trident in the breast. Men and women – children, even – roared with delight when he came out into the area. They beat their breasts and yelled out his name when he killed his enemies, celebrating his victory.

Some victory, Samson thought bitterly. He

was fighting against other slaves, boys just like him conscripted into playing at soldiers for the entertainment of the crowds. Boys just like him, who cried and wept for their mothers at night in their cots, on the hard straw, on the floor if they were unlucky. Hardly the sort of enemy you felt proud about killing. But that was how it was in Rome, in the arena, where the blood spattered on the sand. You killed or you died. And Samson had chosen to live. And live he had – for centuries.

He still remembered the first thing he'd done as a vampire. He'd held his hunger, at first, trained by so many years of hard discipline and militaristic living to ignore his own needs in favor of the ultimate goal. He waited until sunset and then went out into the arena, and waited for the command to kill the boy in front of him, a skinny and terrified thing from Thrace, whose feet got tangled in his fishing net. Oh, Samson had wanted to taste him – the bloodlust was strong within him. He could have given into this strange, new hunger instantly; he could have wrenched the boy's head from his neck and gulped

6

down the blood for those few instants when the heart still beat. But he had a bigger goal in mind. He knew, at last, who his enemy was.

Thousands – that was how many could fit in the arena. Thousands of spectators come to watch one of them die – him or the boy from Thrace. Thousands of shouting, waving. Many of them were his *fans*, people who came back again and again to cheer him on in this horror.

He slaughtered them all with gladiatorial precision. Thousands of them, all at once. His anger was greater than his hunger, but both were sated. The rows of the arena all trickled through with blood. They used sand to get rid of the smell – sand like this desert sand before him. But not all the sand in the Sahara that stretched out before him could have gotten rid of that smell. As Samson looked out at the desert, the sands that stretched level in the distance, he thought once more of the screaming, of the death, of all that he had done, of his rage.

But he was not angry now. His time with Octavius, his time with the Consortium, had

7

stripped the anger from him – both his human and his vampire selves. He had re-learned discipline, learned to fight the good fight. But every now and then he wondered if it was worth it. *Wouldn't it be better if there were no vampires and no humans? If the world were as empty as this desert?*

But there was no time for such philosophical musings. Samson had a mission now. He had to find Octavius, taken into captivity by Nereti and her followers. The vicious Queen had a mission, too – the domination of all the world – and he could not let her win. Samson may, in his darkest dreams, despised the world humans controlled, but deep down he knew Nereti's would be worse.

Nereti, Nereti, he thought. *Will we never be free of you?*

She was the great Queen, worshipped in Egypt as a goddess by many, the great and savage power that struck the most terrible fear into the hearts of men, and the place where hearts might once have been in the vampires that followed her. She was the Great Mother of Death, for so they called her, with

8

her alabaster skin so waxy it made you sick to look at it, and her hair so dark you could lose yourself in looking at it, and her lips so red it reminded you of all the blood you'd shed. She had the greatest power, the darkest power; she overwhelmed and terrified all who were by her side.

Once, Samson had defeated her. Together with Octavius, he and the Consortium had captured Nereti and put her to sleep. It had been almost a thousand years ago that they'd done it – at last won the battles that had slaughtered so many of their men – and they'd thought they'd rid the world of that ancient scourge forever. But now she was back, brought to life again by the cruelty of another's blood. And now she would want revenge.

"You fool," A voice hissed behind him, and he whipped around, his muscles tensed and ready to fight. "You really think that you could evade us forever?" The voice was full of hatred.

Samson's muscles tensed up. He recognized the vampires that surrounded him – all one hundred of them – as Nereti's men. *How had they come up*

9

behind him so quietly? If he had been human, his mouth would have gone dry; strange terror coursed through him. He knew Nereti granted her men strange powers, but this...?

"We're told to take you alive...well, sort of alive, anyway." The vampire grinned through his fangs. "Now, you have two choices. You can come quietly, or you can come...not so quietly..."

It was hopeless; it didn't matter. Samson fought – fought as desperately as he could – killed at least seven or eight of them before it was captured, sent his ruby stake flying through the flesh that turned so quickly to ash.

But they outnumbered him in the end, as he knew they would, and he gave himself over to his surrender.

"We have a very special punishment for you," one laughed, as they held him fast. He would not stop struggling, he told himself – he would fight against this as he fought against all else – raging against their presence, raging against their strength. He was a gladiator, after all, and he knew how to fight. He knew how to kill. But he had never before had to go up against this many vampires alone.

At last they conquered him. They flung his Life's Blood ring from his finger, and one vampire snatched it up greedily. He watched as they dug a hole in the sand, big enough for a beast to fit in; at last they threw him in and packed the earth around him, leaving him scorched and immoble, overcome by the heaviness of the sands.

"Just you wait for dawn, now," leered his conqueror.

So, this was how he was going to die. Samson's heart constricted within his chest. He would not be given the dignity of a good death in battle, a death by the stake or sword. No, he would be slaughtered like a beast, left to die of exposure in these hot and level sands, left to burn. This was Nereti's final revenge, he raged inwardly. She would leave him no victory, no noble death. She would have him die like an animal out there.

"Just fight me properly," he roared. "Fight me, cowards! Kill me!"

11

And then there was silence. The silence of fear. The silence of awe. The silence of unadulterated loyalty. Their leader had arrived.

Among them, a tall woman moved – glided above the sands, her face veiled, but her statue nonetheless striking. She was tall, so tall, and slender, with the muscular bearing of an Amazon of whom he had heard tales of old. She radiated power, emanated force and strength from every element of her being. Samson felt the depths of the old powers rumbling in the desert in answer to her call.

"Nereti!" he cried, his voice spiked with hatred. "Know this! You may have me killed like a dog, but you will never have my honor. You will never see me beg. I will die as befits a soldier."

"Die..." Nereti's voice was soft and slick. "But you are already dead, my brother."

"Will you watch him die, my Queen?" the vampire was slack-jawed.

She unveiled herself.

How beautiful she was, Samson thought, and hated himself for thinking it. The same beautiful

12

sultry eyes, the color of chocolate or burned sienna, with their catlike flecks of golden glow. Her lips, so full and red, that it made you think of the passion you had lost in your mortal years. Her long, dark hair, shimmering in the very hint of dawn, just as beautiful as the legends said she was. And two ruby stakes in her hands.

Rubies.

Samson realized what was happening a split second before the guards did. He was fully aware of what it meant, the fear in their eyes, the recognition.

Without blinking, Nereti slaughtered them all, turning vampire after vampire into mere ash.

Samson gasped.

"You look just like her, you know." His voice was shaking as she began to dig up the sand, freeing him from his desert prison. And then - "I thought you were dead."

"I was," Kalina said. "For a while."

"Then..." a smile spread across his face. The first smile in days. "You are the one in the prophecy. Only one can rise from the dead. Octavius would be

13

so pleased."

He saw the worry in her eyes – and something more than worry. Love? She tried to hide it, but he could smell it out.

"Have you located him?"

Samson nodded. "Yes," he said. "He isn't too far from here." He swallowed. "But I am afraid it will be too late."

Chapter 1

As she stood before Samson on the sands, her feet hovering a few inches above the earth, Kalina felt a strange power she had never known before. The ruby stake still shook in her hands – not because she was trembling with fear, she thought, but because her whole body seemed to be coursing through with new strength. What was she feeling? Every day, Kalina felt, she was rediscovering her body anew, rediscovering her strength, rediscovering what it meant to be a carrier of Life's Blood. The power that she possessed, she knew, was not her own – it was the power of an ancient line of Carriers, of so many before her, so many that had died in the service of protecting the world from vampires. And yet – it was a power more ancient than that. It was a power not unlike that which ran in the veins of the vampire queen Nereti, whom she so resembled.

It had been intoxicating, she thought, her blood running hot with guilt, to see how they had all looked at her, during those brief vain moments when they had mistaken her for their Queen. For she did look like her, didn't she? A resemblance close enough to fool even the most ardent of her worshippers. The same dark hair, deep like a murder of crows. The same caramel-colored skin, blindingly white light glowing out from every pore. The same dark red lips – ruby lips, Kalina thought, like the lips of maidens in a fairy tale. Was this even *her?* The features were ostensibly the same as the ones she had grown up with, but the beauty, the power – all this was new to her. All this was the doing of Life's Blood, the sanguine force that kept surprising her, kept her as a stranger to her own body.

She had let them think she was Nereti. She had felt how they had worshipped her, in those moments. And, although she hated to admit it, even to herself, she had enjoyed it. She had *enjoyed* the adulation, the adoration, the loyalty that in the hearts of less cruel men might even have been called love. Such a thought horrified her.

Kalina thought then of something her mother

16

– no, not her mother, her *adopted* mother, but that didn't sound right – used to say. *There but for the grace of God go I.* She used to say it whenever the family encountered someone who had fallen on old times – the drug-addled homeless man who wandered through the parking lot of their apartment building every now and then, the old woman who slept in the doorways of the local bookstore at night, who had frightened Kalina once when she was a child, and the old woman had told her that her life had been "cursed from the start." *There but for the grace of God go we all,* Kalina's mother used to tell her – meaning that *it could have been any one of us.* Never judge, Kalina's mother always said – treat everyone with compassion. Because only circumstances separated the fortunate from the downtrodden, those who made the right choices and those who chose the wrong path.

Now she thought of it again, as she remembered Nereti's cruel face, how easily she had slaughtered so many young girls, Carriers of Life's Blood that couldn't have been more than children, drained them dry. She thought of her own powers, her own face, the way she had enjoyed the worshipfulness of Nereti's vampires. *There but for the grace of God go I,* she thought.

But she couldn't think about all that now. She had to focus. The dawn was coming, and Samson was still deep within the sands.

"You okay?" Her voice sounded strange to her in a desolate desert like this. It was the sort of desert where you could be silent for a thousand years.

"Let's get me out of this, all right?" Samson's snarl was hardly directed at her, but it stung.

She began digging in the dirt, scooping up handfuls of sand.

"I'm going as fast as I can," she said. "But we may need backup."

"Backup? We're in a bloody desert, Kalina – there's nobody around for miles."

"Get with the times, Samson," she smiled wryly. She pulled out her cell phone and began to dial.

"Two thousand years on this earth," muttered

Samson under his breath, "and there are some things I'll never get used to."

"We've located Octavius," Kalina's voice into the phone was quick, brisk, brusque. "He's not in Egypt any longer. But not *too* far – relatively speaking. We're in the middle of the Sahara now." She sighed softly. "No place for lovers of the shadows, is it? I'll text you our GPS coordinates." She nodded. "Tell the others, okay? Okay, I will." She paused. "I love you too. And be careful." She laughed. "Yes, I'll be careful too, although I can't promise I'll stay put. Octavius is on the move, so we have to be, too."

She continued digging in the dirt, until Samson felt himself free down to the shoulders, stretching his neck.

"Even vampires get cramps," he said.

As Kalina dug, a dark shadow flitted across the sands.

"Well, will you look at that?"

Kalina's heart began to pound faster at the sound of the voice. Familiar – cocksure, full of

19

arrogance, and yet with a good-natured confidence that always sent her reeling with desire. It was Jaegar's voice, and Kalina's heart constricted with longing.

"Not in a million years, I say. Not in a million years would I have expected to see the great gladiator Samson the Strong buried in the sand like a child's toy." He laughed, and his laughter echoed all across the desert. "This gives hope to all us smaller, and dare I say it, trimmer, vampires out there. Don't you think so, Kalina?"

"You're lucky I can't wring your neck right now," Samson snarled. But Kalina could detect a fundamental sheepishness beneath the feigned anger. They were safe, for now, and that was what mattered. "And what were you doing, while I was out on the road, trying to find the oldest and strongest leader of the Consortium? Flirting with girls in bars?"

"Let me guess," Jaegar joked, "you were on the phone with your clingy girlfriend, trying to explain to her that no, you *weren't* having an affair, you *weren't out with another woman,* you had an important job to

20

do if she'd only let you do it, et cetera, et cetera..."

Kalina smiled against herself. Everybody knew about the insecurities of Samson's latest paramour. The girl had once been Octavius' mistress and, though well-intentioned enough, wasn't exactly known for her mental stability.

"Excuses, excuses," Jaegar fell to his knees and began to help Kalina dig Samson out of the sand. Kalina felt his presence next to her – as powerful as an electric shock. How could he make her feel like this, even after all this time? His presence was still wildly intoxicating to her, filling her with a hunger as powerful as bloodlust, driving her mad. She wanted him so badly, now – enough to push him down into the sand and sacrifice all the power of her Life's Blood if it meant being with him as fully, as viscerally, as she wanted to be. She needed him – she *needed him.* But she had to focus on the mission at hand. Octavius was in trouble, and they had to save him.

In a few minutes, the full body of Samson – broad-shouldered and massy – was free of the desert sands.

"Take this ring," Kalina took a Life's Blood ring from where it lay above a pile of vampire ash. "You'll need it."

Samson wiped the sand from his body. "I never thought I'd be saying this," he said gruffly, "but thank you – Kalina, and thank you Jaegar. Credit where credit is due, I suppose."

"Speaking of giving thanks," Kalina replied, "I should be thanking you. You say you know where Octavius is." Her voice faltered, as it always did when she said that name. Was her love for him that obvious, she wondered? Even after all that had happened between them, even after the impossibility of them ever being together, Kalina still felt a wild care for him. He was the one she couldn't have – the one she'd had to give up. And the bitterness of their several partings still stung at her.

"He's strong and smart," Samson said. "Nereti won't break him, I know it."

"Kalina...'" Jaegar's voice was low and urgent, and she saw that there was a darkness in his eyes.

"What is it?" She felt her stomach plummet. "Do you know something I don't?"

"Kal," he brushed her cheek with his fingertips. "Kal, I'm sorry. Nereti...well...you know how she is. She is the most ruthless of vampires, the embodiment of pure evil. She is the worst a vampire can be. And I just want to make sure you're prepared. I just want to make sure you can deal..."

"What are you talking about?" Kalina swallowed down the worry, down the fear. "What's happening to Octavius?" She gulped. "It's bad, isn't it?"

"As a matter of a fact..."

Another voice came up behind her – familiar, too. Max was striding across the sands, Justin by her side.

"Mom?" The word was still strange to her. "How did you and Justin get here so fast?"

"We were already on our way here when you called. There was a major crisis in a nearby town. A whole community of ancient vampires – Octavius' old friends, Consortium associates – were slaughtered."

"No..."

"The thing is..." Max looked worried. "Nobody but Octavius knew where they were. They were hidden – even I didn't know their exact location until I found the ash. I heard the story from one survivor. The only survivor. Five vamps came – wiped out the village completely, vampire and human alike. An inside job."

"You can't mean..."

"Octavius," Jaegar nodded. "She must have turned him."

"No..." Kalina bit back her tears. It couldn't be true – it *couldn't* be! "Octavius would never do that. He'd rather die than rat out his own."

"Maybe he didn't have a choice," Max said.

"What do you mean?"

"Maybe he was tortured. Glamoured. He might not be himself," Jaegar said. "I know you want to see him again, Kalina, but be sure you know what you're looking for. The Octavius you find might not be the one you lost."

She could not deal; she *would* not deal, now.

She would not deal with the tears stinging at her eyes. "Then let's stop wasting time talking here and let's *move*. We need to find him!"

"He's in Morocco," said Max. "Near Fez."

Samson nodded. "That's my intel, too."

Kalina wiped away the tears.

"Then that's where we'll go," she said. "Now!"

Chapter 2

They travelled faster than ever before. Back in the old days, Kalina remembered, she and Justin had to be carried – Stuart and Jaegar and other vampires transporting them in their arms. They'd been slowed down by the extra weight. No longer. Now Kalina could run like a vampire could run, gliding over the sands and the waves of the sea. She was no longer dead weight, a mortal imposition on vampire strength. She was powerful in her own right, fast, not a vampire but a strange hybrid third thing, neither fully mortal nor fully unnatural. And she loved it.

This was her favorite part of Life's Blood, this feeling of power. This feeling that she could keep up with Jaegar and Samson, that she could hold her own, that she no longer had to be protected but indeed was the one doing the protecting. It filled her with excitement, with joy. She was no damsel in distress any longer, she thought gladly. She was a Carrier like her mother, a creature full of power. The feeling was intoxicating, rich, overwhelming. She had been able to fly as a Carrier for some time, but things felt different since her resurrection. Her powers were stronger still as if her brush with death had served as an electric jolt, forcing her into new life.

And a new life it was, Kalina thought, half-bitterly. So much had changed in such a short span of time. Her dreams of college, of a normal life, were not merely postponed – in all likelihood they would be put off forever. Stuart remained with Maeve at his side at the Greystone Winery in Rutherford, California, helping to fend off any vampire attacks or incidents in town. Kalina had brought some of the Carriers they had saved from Nereti's sacrifice there. Many of them were too young to be able to protect themselves, but some of the older ones had begun to awaken to their strength. Like Sydney. Dark-eyed and hollow-cheeked, Sydney was the oldest of the Carriers to have survived Nereti's purges, and the memory of what she had seen, what she had been through, haunted her always. But she used her frustration, her rage, as a means to an end: she was constantly demanding to be taught more, to learn more – how to spot vampires, how to fight like vampires, how to kill them. "I want them all turned to ash," Sydney had said, much to Stuart's chagrin. Stuart, who had the knowledge and experience of a vampire even while mortal, was the perfect tutor for them. But his guilt about his old life still remained.

And of course Justin. Newly turned, Justin was going through a different kind of trauma. Poor Justin, Kalina thought mournfully. He had always been the normal one, the sane one, the *human* one, clinging to his normalcy. He hadn't wanted any special talents. He hadn't wanted any special powers. He had just wanted to go about his business, spending time with the family and friends he loved, keeping them all safe. And now he was forced to live forever as a vampire, walking the earth as a creature he despised, knowing all the while that Carriers like Sydney looked upon him with hatred and fear because of that hunger he was not sure he could bring himself to control. Every day was a struggle for him. Justin and Max flew silently at Kalina's side.

But Kalina couldn't think about that now. She had a new concern to occupy her – the fate of Octavius. He was in captivity, now, held by Nereti and her vampire army. And she did not even dare to think about what Nereti might be doing to him. What tortures, what glamours, might this most powerful of all vampire queen know? How might she try to break him, to make him her creature? And if what the others said were true... No...Kalina could not bring herself to think the words! Octavius *could not* have been responsible for the massacre near Fez! He could not have been responsible for all those deaths, the slaughter of his beloved friends, his allies. Octavius was a soldier, he was a man of honor – he was the most honorable being, man or vampire, that she knew. He would never...

And yet when they arrived at that village, sand blowing across the dunes, Kalina felt the chill that meant only one thing. Death. All the houses were

29

empty; ash was scattered on every threshold. And Kalina felt something more than that, more palpable than that. The feeling of death was all around her, searing into her skin. She swallowed, gulped, forced herself to hold back the tears. It was as if the dying vampires had left some sort of psychic mark here, memorializing their own deaths. The air was full of ghosts. The ghosts of majestic, ancient vampires, as noble and as powerful as Octavius, his loyal peers.

His victims?

"What happened here?" Kalina felt her voice quivering. What did she expect, she asked herself? Did she expect the walls to answer her?

Samson sniffed the air. "Murder," he said darkly. "Murder most foul."

"A surprise attack." Jaegar looked down, and they all watched as the dune winds blew away the last of the dusty footprints in the cave. "I've heard of this place, Kal. The cave – there was a reason that the vampires chose it."

"What do you mean?"

"It held precious treasure," Samson cut in.

"Treasures deemed priceless to vampires. So the Consortium members here met to guard it."

"What kind of treasure?" Kalina asked him. What kind of treasure could possibly be important enough for vampires to devote their entire existence to guarding it?"

Samson looked down at his feet, shuffling. He seemed distinctly uncomfortable, grunting harshly. If vampires could blush, Kalina thought, he'd be blushing now. "You tell her," he snapped, turning to Jaegar.

Jaegar looked confused at first, but Samson gave him a pointed look. "Oh. *Oh.*" He looked at Max and Justin. "I need to tell you in private, Kalina. Let's go for a short walk, shall we?"

Kalina was uncertain. "It'd have to be fast, Jaegar. I really don't like knowing that Nereti is fully awakened, that her power is restored. She's out there – she wants revenge – she has Octavius, and..."

Jaegar grabbed her arm and started walking, yanking her alongside with him. "We'll be back shortly," he called over his shoulder to the others.

31

"Try to see if you can't find out anything else about what's going on."

No sooner were they out of sight, deep within the labyrinthine cave, than he pushed her up against the cavern wall, pushing her arms up above her head, kissing her wildly, passionately. "Oh, Kal," he murmured. "You have no idea how much, how long, I've wanted to do that. Oh, how I've been waiting for you. Not a word – no notice – nothing to say. You simply...got up from the dead, took a shower, ate, grabbed your stakes, and said "let's go." You said 'let's go to Octavius' and left us in the dust." Bewilderment and pain crossed his face, but Kalina could still see the unmistakable impression of love and desire.

"I mean...after all we've been through! After you put me through the grief of seeing you dead, you could at least have spent some time safe at home. Letting me hold you. Letting me touch you. Letting me take you, getting as close as we could get to bringing our bodies together." He groaned aloud. "I barely got a chance to touch you before you were off.

Tell me, Kalina, what happened?"

Kalina shook her head, trying mournfully to explain. "Things are different now," she tried. They were different – now that she realized how limited was the time she had. Dying had clarified things in her mind. Made her realize how important it was to stop Nereti before she carried out her plans of destruction. "Jaegar," she gently touched his face. "Believe me, I love you. I love you so much, and sometimes I think there's nothing I want more than to let you have your way with me. But it's like – when I died and came back, ever since then all I've been able to think about was stopping Nereti. I keep thinking -that must be why I've been given another shot at life, when all those other Carriers died. To stop her. And I can't fall short of the mission now."

"It was whatever was in that vial your mother gave you to drink – the miracle blood or whatever it was...from the doctor's box we found in China." Jaegar took a step back. "What else is different now? Besides the gliding, the faster flying, what else have you noticed is different?"

"I've been single-minded," Kalina admitted. "About Nereti. But also..." It felt good to admit it out loud. "My...desires. They've been stronger, lately." It was true. Her vampire strength had brought with it a new vampire hunger – a new desire she could not control. "This." She pushed Jaegar back against the wall, twisting him around to hold him off the floor, raising her lips higher until they were brushing the top of his jeans. She unbuckled his belt, slid it off, unbuttoned his jeans, feeling beneath the denim the hard force of him, waiting with desire for her. She would have to give in, now – now that he had awakened it. Her desires were too strong for her to bear.

"Kal..." Jaegar put a warning hand on his shoulder. "That vision of you just now is something I want to cherish for the rest of my life – your mouth...there..." Jaegar closed his eyes, shuddering. "But I can't. Not here."

"You think it'll destroy the Life's Blood?" Kalina's voice was rough with desire.

"No – I think the rules are pretty

34

straightforward," Jaegar said. "But....when we do go that bit further, I want to do it right, Kalina. I want to do it to you, too."

"No!" Kalina's aggression surprised her. "No..." She laughed softly. "Funny. Ever since I woke up from the dead...I've been feeling...like I want to conquer. Take everything. Like I want to go after what I want. Like...I want every man here to submit to me. Like Nereti."

Jaegar's eyes lit up, and a wickedly wide smile shot across his face. "I like how you take charge, Kal!"

"I'm not so sure..." she admitted. "I'm not sure what it means."

She slowly let Jaegar slide down the wall while she ran her tongue up from his navel to his chest, letting her lips linger on his. He captured her kiss, kissing her back with a wild hunger. In the heat of his passion his fangs appeared, sharp against his lips.

He jumped back and took a deep breath.

"I'm sorry, Kal. I'm having a hard

35

time...keeping my cool..."

She smiled softly. "Keeping your cool, yeah." She knew as well as he that if they were in a nice bed, in their own bed, with all the time in the world, she would submit to him. They would not be able to hold themselves back.

She said nothing, but deep down she knew she was having a hard time keeping her cool, too. This new awakening had brought with it a new hunger. But was it a hunger she could control?

Chapter 3

What was going on? Kalina felt heated, flushed, pink and hot with desire as never before. A few moments ago, all she had been able to think about was her mission, her need to find Octavius and destroy Nereti, no matter what the cost. But now something new, something strange, something utterly foreign to her, had come over her. It was desire, but not like desire as she had known it before. That desire was something she had gotten used to – a mortal, human need. This was something different. Wild like bloodlust, it was – an animal hunger that threatened to take over her, to consume her, to make her its slave. All she wanted to do was make Jaegar submit to her, bodily; in mind too, make him her creature. Deep down some rational part of her tried to fight the desire. *This is crazy, you* *have work to do, you love Jaegar, you don't want to conquer him....*but these small sounds were lost amid the pulsing of her Life's Blood in her veins. Suddenly it was as if nothing in the world mattered but this desire. They walked back to the cave, and Kalina felt the blood so hot within her. Her face was flushed, she knew; Jaegar could read the desire on her face. All of her senses were alert; all of her nerve endings were fired up.

What are you doing, Kalina, this is crazy...

She was hyper-sensitive to his touch. Every brush of his skin against hers, every hint of his flesh so near her flesh, sent her into a wild ecstasy. She could smell him, too – a distinctive vampire smell, the sweet and musky smell of danger, of manhood, of power. She wanted nothing more than to tear off his clothes, rip them from his glistening, taut chest and lick every part of his body, take him and taste him...

"Jaegar..." Her blush grew hot upon her face as she looked down. "Jaegar, please, I can't wait..." Her voice trembled. "If I don't satisfy this right now, I'm..."

Jaegar's hand was tight upon her shoulders. "What are you saying?" His growl was low and throaty.

"I need you, Jaegar," she whispered.

His brow furrowed at first in concern and confusion, but as the full force of her words struck him his expression gave way to one of joy and deep desire.

"What are you saying?"

"I need you *now.*"

"We have to go back to the others," he forced out, his voice husky with need. "We need to..."

She was hot – so hot – her skin burning, her face burning, her whole body burning for him. She could not stop herself from kissing his neck, his shoulders, pressing her tongue lightly against his chest underneath his shirt.

"Kalina," he groaned. "Oh, Kalina...wait...I'll tell the others you decided to break for the night. We'll go to a hotel, check us all in...get a room to ourselves..." His voice trembled and he could not finish the sentence.

He went back to the others inside the cave, leaving Kalina alone. Sweat pearled upon her body. Inside, she was burning with lust. What was happening?

Then he had returned, quickly telling Samson and the rest that Kalina was overcome with a side effect of her resurrection and needed to get out of there fast and to the closest hotel to rest. So, in record time, without question because everyone didn't know what to expect with Kalina coming back to life, they packed up and flew – at vampire speed – to the nearest hotel. It all happened in such a flash.

"Kalina..." Max said, trying to feel Kalina's forehead. "You look alright, but your eyes... they're glazed over and overly wide like you're seeing something. You have a... obsessed look." Max looked over at Jaegar, who was looking everywhere else besides Max's eyes. Almost like some vampire beau who was a little embarrassed to be in the same room with the mom of the woman he was about to deflower.

"Um," he coughed. "Yeah. Kal got that look

when I took her for a walk just now. I think she's remembering a few things from the past, and...well, I think I can help her with that. You know. It must be traumatic waking up from the and finding out you suddenly have this intense craving... Oh," he blushed, his eyes widening. "I know exactly how she feels. It's like when I became a vampire. When I turned. She must be going through some transformation or something, but not quite a full-fledge vampire, but still human but with vampire needs."

"Um, Jaegar," Kalina came up to him and grabbed the front of his crotch, when Max had looked over at the hotel's front registration desk clerk and asked how much longer until they can check in. "I can't wait," Kalina said. "Please hurry this up."

Jaegar swallowed hard, and gritted his teeth. "I'm trying..." He walked up to the desk clerk and looked him in the eyes. "We need a room now. The nicest ones you have, and send us room service with the best dishes from your restaurant in about an hour. Hurry."

The clerk couldn't stop looking at Jaegar's mesmerizing blue eyes as he nodded and said, "Yes, sir, right away. I have the entire penthouse floor for you and your guests. Complements of the hotel, Sir Greystone."

Jaegar nearly shoved everyone into their own rooms as soon as they got up to the penthouse suite floor and grabbed Kalina, pulling her into his suite, covered in luxurious fabrics – silks and satins and damask. The large bed lay covered in silk, furs, and soft pillows beckoned to them, and they fell together into bed, their arms and legs intertwined, in a single heated embrace.

She had forgotten why they had visited the cave...what was their mission. She was consumed by an unquenchable thirst for power, over Jaegar, over anyone, over everyone, but especially first over the very vampires who should serve her.

"What has come over you?" Jaegar whispered, as she tore off his jeans. "Whatever it is, they should bottle it up and sell it to all women. A guy likes a woman to take charge like this once in a while. So sexy."

"Quiet," Kalina said, impatiently pulling off her own jeans. Soon they had stripped to their underwear. His chest – so muscular, so pale like ivory – glimmered in the evening light. And she...she looked different too. Kalina looked down at her body – it had changed, somehow. She was shapelier, somehow – more tanned, more toned, more beautiful than ever before. She stood up straighter, admiring her shapelier, stronger, and more womanly body. The woman in the mirrored walls around the bed looked confident, radiant, and hungry with desire. In all her haste in running from and chasing vampires ever since the death of her first boyfriend Aaron, the half-brother to Stuart and Jaegar, she haven't taken the time to look at herself. It had been nearly three years now, and she was no longer a naïve teen girl but a woman who would be twenty soon...an adult, a new adult, but still someone who could be old enough to get married, have children, and *conquer the world...starting with this vampire.*

"Like an Egyptian queen," Jaegar whispered

into her flesh as he came up behind her and kissed her shoulder. "My very own Egyptian queen. You are so beautiful, Kalina..." He kneeled to the floor before her while she sat upon the bed watching him, pulsing with desire, stripped by now down to her panties. "So gloriously beautiful." He kissed her inner thighs before moving up to face her, his mouth curling in a wicked smile as he prepared to taste, her, to savor her – oh, Kalina could not bear the waiting!

"Let's get this out of the way, shall we?" He winked at her before tearing the crotch of her panties from her, his vampire fangs slicing through the black lace fabric. "That's better."

And then he was kissing her there, his tongue smooth and hungry against her heated flesh. She could not stop herself from moaning in ecstasy, from crying out loud in sheer pleasure, her back arched, her hair falling back against the pillow, until she too had thrown her whole body back on the bed, with Jaegar's head and tongue still buried between her thighs. They had fooled around before, but never like

44

this. The feelings, the pleasure, the pain – the *need* were all heightened. She had never felt such pleasure before. She shuddered with each new wave of touch. "What's happening?"

Jaegar raised his head, grinning, his absence from her inner thighs tormenting her. "Maybe this is a new vampire ability – or a vampire curse. Every hunger is heightened. Even this one. I've never been with anyone like this before, Kal. The sensation, the pleasure – it's unbelievable..."

"I'm beginning to understand why they say vampires can't hold back," Kalina struggled to force out the words between moans.

"It's why we equate sex with feeding, Kal. The two things that make us vampires feel alive. Stronger. More powerful." He moved his mouth up, kissing his way up on her stomach, her ribs, her breasts – so sensitive by now that the slightest touch sent her reeling. He was tormenting her, she know, making her wait for her pleasure, and the mix of desire and desperation she felt sent her all but over the edge.

Blood Curse (Pulse #8)

"Jaegar, I can't wait a moment longer," Kalina cried. "We need to be together now, fully, completely – I don't care about the consequences anymore. I have to be with you. I've already been with you in my mind – take me bodily, too."

"But...the Life's Blood..." Jaegar groaned in frustration and pulled back. "You know we can't, Kal, as much as we want to. We need to fulfill the prophecy. We can't risk de-activating your blood. Now more than ever."

"It's a *stupid* rule!" Kalina cried. "It doesn't even make *sense!*"

"We should stop...." Jaegar looked pained. "I don't want to, Kal, but it'll be harder to stop later, and I'm afraid I'll lose control..."

But even as he backed away from her, Kalina could still feel the pangs of intense sexual pleasure coursing through her, even though Jaegar was standing a few feet away. She could still feel the touch of a tongue lapping between her thighs; still feel fingers brushing against her skin. Was it her own hands...or...

Suddenly the world around her changed. She was no longer in a hotel room, but in a darkened chamber, candle-lit, luxuriously decked out in silks and velvets. The sort of place, she thought, that was fit for a Queen. She was naked, covered in scented oils, fingers rubbing up and down her skin. Magnificent, masculine strong fingers, massaging the tensions out of her thighs, then touching her gently below until she was moaning....

"You have a strong touch, like a lion, but you can be so gentle – like a dove," she heard herself say to the invisible hands. "Hands that have slaughtered many," she continued. "But hands that have made many a woman moan."

"Yes, my Queen." The voice was familiar – too familiar.

"You did well," Kalina was saying now. "This morning. Leading my men to your friends. They never suspected what would happen..."

"A complete surprise." Now she could feel the man's mouth, kissing, licking the golden tanned legs that stretched out towards her beautiful, flawless back. He kneaded her smooth buttocks, and Kalina felt herself inhale sharply with pleasure.

"Lovely," she said.

He continued kneading her flesh, drawing out moans

"You've come a long way in such a short time," Kalina heard herself say. "I'm proud of you. No wonder they revered you so strongly as a general in your day, friend and foe alike." She turned around, kissing him on the mouth, her tongue delving deep, kissing him until he was out of breath. "I am very happy with your progress, my new General. We have the vials your ancient friends guarded so bravely in the cave. Pity that they did not even save what they lay down their lives for. We will keep these hidden in our possession until the time comes when we will need them."

She looked down at Octavius' smooth muscles, his taut stomach, his sinewy legs, and moved up close to him. She tore the loin-cloth from his hips, sighing with delight as she took in his naked body before her. "You are magnificent," she

48

proclaimed, licking her lips. "For the attack, for retrieving these vials, for giving me such pleasure, you deserve a reward. Well done, Octavius, well done."

She bent down and took his hardness into her, moving her lips and tongue so skillfully that soon Octavius was crying out with intense pleasure, her whole body, like his, shuddering with release...

"Nereti," he cried. "Nereti, my Queen...."

And then Kalina's eyes flew wide open, and she shot back up, screaming, screaming, and screaming his name.

"What is it?" Jaegar flew to her side. "What happened?"

"A dream...no, no, it wasn't a dream. I saw him...saw him..."

"Who?"

"Octavius. And he was with *her!*"

"Nereti?" Jaegar looked concerned.

"Yes, he was with her. I mean, *with. Her.*"

"That's impossible," Jaegar looked shocked. "Octavius loves only you, you know that."

"He was the one who led the attack – it's true – I heard her say it...."

"Then it's not really him," Jaegar insisted. "Nereti's glamours are powerful. She's controlled him, brain-washed him into forgetting who he really is. Octavius, the Octavius I know – the Octavius I constantly try to compete with... - he never would hurt you like that. The real Octavius would stake himself before doing her will."

He wrapped his arms around Kalina, who tried – tried and failed! - To hold back her tears. "You know it doesn't mean he doesn't love you, Kal. He loves you so much – and even in my envy I can never deny it. He loves you so much....but now...he is forced to serve another."

50

Chapter 4

Kalina couldn't believe it. Could this really be happening to her? She had never once doubted Octavius' love, Octavius' strength. He had been the powerful one, the forceful one, the one that she could trust even when she could not trust herself. Kalina remembered with bitterness how often she had been the one to try to overcome his scruples, to make him give into temptation, to overflow with desire until all his professed self-denial was for naught. How often had she offered herself to him, stretched out her naked body before him so that he might take her all in and gasp at her beauty; how often had she placed his cold hands against the warmth of her breasts and begged him to want her – begged him to give in? He was so strong – she had always known that! Too strong, she had said. He told her it was a challenge, a struggle, an internal war against his darker impulses, but it was a war he had always won. He had not touched her the way she ached and craved to be touched in months. He had not kissed her properly in almost as long. He had told her the truth – *we can never be together. I must serve my purpose for eternity.* And such a purpose precluded love.

Love – love – love – all her strength and all her power had gone into such love. And it still had been far from enough to make him bend to her will. It had still been far from enough to make him touch her, to make him *want* her as violently and uncontrollably as she wanted him. Kalina had tried to seduce Octavius so many times, so *very* many times, and every single time she had failed.

But Nereti had succeeded.

The bitterness made Kalina want to vomit. What she had failed to do – Nereti had succeeded! She had overcome his scruples, his power, his desire to do good. His lust and need for *her* had been enough to destroy everything he held dear. He had betrayed his friends, his Consortium allies, his principles, his *loves.*

*No...*Kalina raged inwardly. *He never loved*

52

you, Kalina. This whole time that you thought, you imagined, you dreamed that he wanted you, loved you, you were wrong. The reason he was able to withstand you had nothing to do with nobility or strength. It had nothing to do with any of it at all. The only reason he withstood your advances was because he didn't want you enough.

Not like her.

Not like her.

How could she have been so stupid? Kalina felt the hot tears dribbling down her face. Nereti was an ageless vampire queen, befitted with all the powers her station deserved, powers of seduction and glamour that no human, not even a Life's Blood Carrier, could rival. Nereti was more beautiful than she was – in the darkest recesses of her heart Kalina felt sure that this was the truth. Older, more experienced, more seductive. She knew how to please a man – or a vampire.

No, Kalina felt sure of it – Octavius had never loved her. He had felt sorry for her; he had pitied her; he had told her a kind excuse in order to let her down easy, rather than revealing the truth about how he really felt.

That was how it was! The tears were coming faster now, so quickly that she did not bother to wipe them away on the silken sheets of the hotel suite. They were boiling on her vampire-cool skin.

"Kalina, please..." Jaegar was wrapping his arms around her, enveloping her in the kind strength of his embrace. "Kalina, please don't cry. I can't stand to see you like this. I can't stand to see you hurting." He swallowed hard. "And I admit it – I'm jealous, too. Seeing you get worked up like this over him."

"I thought he loved me!" she cried. "I thought...I'm so stupid, Jaegar..."

"He *does* love you..." Jaegar stroked her hair. "That's what makes it so hard to hate him, to be jealous of him, even though I want to. If I thought he didn't deserve your love, I'd have staked him long ago, even though he's my Maker. His love for you is as strong as mine – as strong as Stuart's. His love for you was what brought us to you long ago. It's only a

54

spell, darling. Only some sort of enchantment."

"How can you be sure?"

"You saw what was happening, didn't you? A dream?"

"I saw...everything..." How could she explain what she had seen! Nereti's ruby-red lips closing around Octavius' shining, hard manhood – their faces contorted by pleasure, the moment of release when Octavius called the name that was not her own...

"You were only able to see that because of your telepathic connection with Octavius. A connection that is a strong proof of love. You know that, Kal. Be strong, my darling. You have to be strong – for me, for him. We're never going to save him if you don't have faith that he can be saved."

"But does he *want* to be saved?" Kalina heard herself snap. "Or does he want to spend the rest of eternity with *her*..."

"He doesn't, Kal darling, I'm sure of it."

"I could feel his pleasure. I could feel how much he was enjoying it. And I could feel *hers*, too!

Could feel how much *she* wanted him...could feel how much *she* needed him."

"Wait, what?" Jaegar's brow furrowed in concern. "You felt *her*?"

"Yes," Kalina sniffled. "I felt both of them. Him and her. Looking through his eyes at hers, her eyes at him."

"Her eyes at him?"

"Yeah, what does it matter?"

"Kal..." Jaegar's voice dropped low. "This is serious, Kal. Like, really serious."

"What are you talking about?" Kalina couldn't even bear to look up. She wanted to forget him, forget everything, forget her pain. She didn't want to talk about this a second longer than she had to – she was not sure if she could bear it.

"You're connected...to *her*." Jaegar let the words sink in. "You're connected to Nereti. If you can experience what she experiences, if you can feel what she feels, that means the two of you are..."

"I do *not* have a telepathic connection with Nereti!" Kalina shouted. "I hate her – I despise her..."

"But you're linked," Jaegar said, holding her hands tighter. "I don't know how and I don't know why, but I know that it's true. The two of you have a bond that transcends space and time. You're connected to her. If you can feel what she feels." He gazed into her eyes. "What did Nereti say? You have insight, Kalina. This is valuable."

"I don't *want* to hear her thoughts!"

"But it could help us, Kal," insisted Jaegar. "It could save us."

"I don't know..." Kalina flung up her hands in despair. "Something about...I don't know...something about vials."

"Vials?"

"This precious treasure – whatever they had in the caves – she's got possession of them. She's controlling them now."

"She has the vials?" Jaegar's face fell.

"What's in those vials?"

"It's the treasure I told you about. The one that most vampires have heard about only in legend." Against Jaegar looked uncomfortable, even embarrassed. "The vampire seed."

"Seed? What do you mean seed?" It hit her all at once. "Oh...you mean?"

"Yeah."

"*Ew!*"

"Like I said, it's a little uncomfortable...."

"Vampires, normal vampires, cannot procreate. They cannot produce offspring the normal way – with a human, as opposed to turning a vampire. They're taken by newborn vampires right before or right after a turning – to maintain fertility."

"*Ew!*" It was Kalina's turn to feel uncomfortable. "But what could Nereti possibly want with *that*? Her vampires have all turned long ago. What could she be planning to do with them?"

"I don't know," Jaegar grimaced. "But whatever it is, it's not good. These caves – these secret chambers – have been the repository of vampire fertility, vampire sexuality, for centuries. They used to call this place the Blood-Womb."

"The Blood-Womb," Kalina sniffed. "Sounds a bit creepy." She looked up. "This place...the repository of vampire sexuality."

"It's meant to have...certain powers."

"And what just happened with us?" Kalina remembered the wild, uncontrollable hunger that had taken over her body and mind for a few hours, that which had caused her to forget the plan, forget the mission, rush straight into a hotel room, into Jaegar's arms, into Jaegar's bed.

"You mean..."

"Was that...supernatural?"

Jaegar laughed softly. "It *felt* supernatural."

"No, I mean – was that *us*?"

"It was amazing, wasn't it? That passion? That desire, seeping through us, overcoming us, making us wild..."

"No!" Kalina heard herself cry. "No!" Had she been glamour into desire – no less than Octavius had? Was love, was desire, so easily won, that magic could control her body and mind? A few seconds ago she'd been freaking out about Octavius' glamouring – now, she realized, she had come far closer to glamouring than she might once have believed.

"You enjoyed it, didn't you?"

"Yes..." Kalina admitted. "But...we weren't in control."

"We were *out of control.*"

"Something – some *force* – took over us!" She tried to explain how she felt – how strangely violated the knowledge made her feel. "Made us want to – even when we had something more important to worry about. Just like Nereti and Octavius!"

"It's not like that, Kal..."

He leaned over to touch her, but she pulled away. As much as she wanted him, wanted his hands on her, wanted his flesh so close and strong against hers, she couldn't let it happen again. Not when she wasn't sure whether it was she who was doing the wanting, or the mysterious magic of the caves.

"I want you, Jaegar," her voice was husky with desire. "I want you so badly. But I don't trust myself. So much power is all around us. Even without the vials, the Blood-Womb has exerted a powerful force over us. And I don't want to do something because

I'm drunk with lust for you, drunk with hunger. I want to do something when I'm sure I'm in my own mind."

"I'm never in my own mind when I'm around you," whispered Jaegar hoarsely.

"I don't know who controls my mind anymore," Kalina whispered, her voice shaking. The Blood-Womb, Nereti, her telepathic connections with those she loved – her mind was not her own. It was a whirlpool of voices, images, needs, desires – things she could not control. How was she meant to bear it – any of it? How was she meant to separate herself from the echoes of so many others who were connected to her by blood?

"All I know is, Jaegar, I'm scared. For the first time, I'm really scared. And I don't know what to do next."

Chapter 5

Jaegar furrowed his brow. Kalina could see the pain in his eyes, a pain that gave a dark cast to his entire countenance. She ached that she had hurt him so. She knew as well as he did his love for her. She knew as well as he did how much he loved her, how much he wanted her, how much he wished – hope against hope – that he might be the only one she loved. Sometimes she wished she could feel that way, too – that the impossibility of her desire might flame itself into true and certain love. But her lusts, her desires, the heat of her blood, were too powerful for her to control. Ever since she had awakened into her status as a Life's Blood Carrier, she had known deep down that she would not be satisfied with one man, one love, a single devotion. Her blood, so full of longing, was meant for something more passionate – it could not be sated by a single kiss, a single adoration. And so too it could not be sated by Jaegar, Jaegar *alone*, however much she might want him. She desired Octavius, too, and Stuart – desired them all with a desire so great she could not bear it.

Oh, it may have been the Blood-Womb that stoked her senses for her, whetting her appetites into something she could neither control nor bear – but Kalina knew that it was something else, too – another force serving to boil her blood. Her connection with Nereti had only made the Life's Blood stronger. It had only increased her lusts, the animal hunger that made her *need* Jaegar's body, Octavius' body, even Stuart's body, the way vampires needed blood. Her enforced virginity – a technicality, she thought bitterly, at this point – felt like a prison. How she wanted to give herself over completely to the longing that subsumed her! How she wanted to feel the purity of her desires fulfilled! She wondered if that would cure her.

After all, she knew, Life's Blood was no longer effective in the same way once the Carrier was no longer a virgin – a *technical* virgin. Would that also cool her longings? Would the desire become manageable again? If she had sex with Jaegar – or Octavius – or Stuart – would she get it out of her system and become....

...what? Normal? Kalina could have scoffed at the words. She was hardly normal, animal desires or no. A Life's Blood Carrier, a vampire in so many ways, human in others – belonging to neither of those two worlds. An eternal wanderer with a price upon her head. And now...linked psychically to a woman she despised. No, Kalina decided mournfully, she would never be normal, whatever else she was. And yet...she couldn't stop thinking about what it would mean to lose her virginity. Would she be free, at last, from the distractions all around her, the desires that thundered in her head and threatened to drive her mad? Would she at last be able to look at Jaegar without becoming overwhelmed by her need to jump him, pressing plan or no pressing plan?

Would she be able to love *someone* – one person – not many? Would she be able to stop breaking the hearts of so many handsome, kind men

64

that deserved better than being her second- or third choice? Would her Life's Blood finally choose someone for her?

"You're so good to me, Jaegar," she whispered. "I don't deserve you."

"You deserve everything," Jaegar pressed her hands to his lips. "You deserve to be happy, and to be with somebody who makes you happy."

"You're so loyal, so good..."

"Funny," Jaegar laughed. "There were centuries when nobody would agree with you there. I was a bad boy, Kalina – *really* bad news. The ones I didn't kill, I still ravished. I seduced country girls, milkmaids, princesses, countesses – with my cock between their legs and my fangs deep in their necks. I was hardly the doting puppy then. But with you...it's out of control. I've met my match. My equal. And perhaps the devotion I feel now is a kind of punishment. I know what it feels like now to be one of my conquests, one of the hearts I've broken. And maybe...." his voice cracked. "Maybe one day someone will break your heart, really break it, and

65

then you'll know too..."

But Kalina's heart *had* been broken. The sight, the smell, the *taste* of Octavius on Nereti's body – all this had already shattered her so deeply she could not bear it. She knew, in the darkness without herself, that her heart existed only in pieces, now. She loved Octavius – how strongly she had not realized – and Octavius had broken her heart.

"Listen to me, Kalina," Jaegar kissed her lightly. "You have to go back."

"Go back where?"

"The dream. The vision. You have a connection with Nereti. You can use it. You can use it to our advantage. If you can gain insight into where she is, what she's thinking, what she's planning, you can use it to stop what she's got up her sleeve..."

"You want me to...relive that?" The idea of it repulsed her. To live once more in Nereti's head, to experience once more the heartbreak of watching the man she loved lick and suck upon and kiss the body of another woman – how could she bear that?

"I know it hurts, Kal. I know how hard it must be. But it's the only way. It's the only way for us to do this. You have a connection none of the rest of us has – and you need to use it."

"Jaegar, I can't!" she wanted to scream. "I can't go back there..."

"You can," a familiar-sounding voice echoed from the doorway. "Honey, I heard everything." Max sauntered in. "Super-strength hearing, remember?"

Jaegar flushed scarlet.

"Listen, I know you don't want to do this. I know it's tough. But you have to be stronger than this. There is much that is more pressing than love in this world. Like children not getting slaughtered. Like a world free from vampire domination. You don't have the luxury of deciding you can't bear this."

"But, Mom..."

"Don't *but Mom* me," Max was stern now. "You know what you have to do. And my heart breaks for you, really it does. But no daughter of mine will let her feelings get in the way of her mission. You know what you have to do. Be strong."

"But what if I can't?"

"Do it anyway."

Max's voice was firm and harsh. But deep down, Kalina knew that she was right. She would have to suffer, have to bear her suffering, have to get through this on her own. Max had survived the world of vampires for so long by putting her own feelings aside. It was the way of the Carrier. Especially one chosen to be the Queen's equal.

That night, in bed, alone, Kalina began to dream of Nereti again. Images flitted before her, flickering like old silent films, images of death and destruction, of slaughter and misery, images of the horrors of the past. Kalina could see it all – the birth of Nereti's empire of destruction, the vampiric hordes that would come to swallow them all up...slaughtering their way to world domination. Kalina knew that she was remembering all that Nereti remembered – the *good old days,* as she called them -when she had slaughtered whole regions of vampires, whole cities of humans, provinces laid to waste and transformed into dust and ash...and

68

blood. That was what she wanted now, Kalina knew. To relive those days, to regain those hours, to rebirth anew that empire of chaos which she had so adored. With Octavius as her consort, Octavius as her prince, Octavius by her side, every bit as wicked as she.

Kalina's stomach lurched. She was sickened by the thoughts. How could she bear to watch such horrors – watch such atrocities? Children killed and drained dry before their parent's eyes, their screams choking out from the bloody gurgles in their throat. Mothers sobbing as their husbands and family were slaughtered, one by one, their blood dripping from vampire fangs. She wanted to vomit, to wake up from this nightmare and scream, scream, scream aloud. But she knew that she could not. She had to bear this – hope that in the depths of this nightmare she might find the key to Nereti's weakness. She knew that Nereti was indestructible – that she had already drank several Life's Blood Carriers to death, draining their power. She knew that Nereti had nearly drained Kal herself. The effects of Life's Blood on her were even stronger than that which Mal had, or the worst Life's Blood vampire had ever experienced.

She had to face this.

But what was worse, still, than the atrocity was the pleasure. As Nereti, she *felt* Octavius' body hard against her own, she felt the pleasure Nereti felt when he buried his tongue between her legs, when he licked and nipped at and bit down upon her inner thigh, making her scream with a mix of ecstasy and pain. She felt the strange satisfaction Nereti felt when she pressed her lips against Octavius' gleaming manhood, felt the power that lay in making him come violently. And she felt, too, what it felt like to have Octavius thrust deep within her, the intimacy that she could never really experience, transmitted to her through the body of another. She felt herself so full, so violently full, of him; felt every inch of her body screaming with pleasure as Octavius drove himself deep within Nereti's body.

It was this experience that was the most confusing of all. She felt disgust, anger, rage that Octavius was doing this – servicing another woman, making love to her. And yet she felt such bizarre pleasure, as if it were *she* experiencing his lips, his hands, his tongue, his cock. In Nereti's body, feeling with Nereti's own nerve endings, she could feel that which she had always longed to feel – feel the force so powerful within her.

And she had to admit – it felt so unbelievably good.

Chapter 6

Kalina found that she could not stop. At first, the idea of entering Nereti's headspace, of becoming Nereti, of reliving her world, had been anathema to her – the very idea had made her sick, made her gorge rise with impossible nausea. At first, she'd wanted to run away and throw up into the desert sands at the very idea. But things were different now. Kalina found herself aching, longing, to return to the dream; she found herself anxiously wanting to go back to that world. A world where she could at last know the pleasure that she so eagerly sought, the pleasure that had for so long eluded her. She craved Octavius; she craved his flesh, she craved his body; she craved his manhood inside her. And at last, inside the body of another, she had known that incredible feeling: that feeling of fullness, of completion, of hunger sated, of thirst slaked, of desire fulfilled and yet made new again. She had felt that which for so long she had longed to feel – the hunger that had been denied her. Until now.

She didn't admit it to Max or to Justin or to Jaegar. She didn't admit it to anybody. How could she? How could she admit that she was not only surviving, she was *enjoying* her dreams of Nereti and Nereti's life? The very thing seemed impossible. She hated Nereti; she despised her world; the very sight of Octavius, his eyes blazing, his lips pressed between Nereti's legs as she arched her back and howled with pleasure, broke her heart in two. And yet the pleasure kept her coming back – the pleasure of feeling Octavius' hands, fingers, lips, tongue, mouth, his hard body against and around her. That pleasure kept her addicted to the world of her dreams. Even when awake, Kalina found, her body still shuddered and shivered with aftershock, with the glow of pleasure sustained even after the moment of orgasm. Even when awake, she could smell Octavius on her; she could smell that heady mix of must and perfume that marked the moment of their union. It felt good – too good. She was addicted to such a pleasure, such a feeling. All she wanted was for it to last forever.

What's happening to you, Kal?

Once she had been a normal sixteen-year-old girl, a girl like every other. A girl in full control of her faculties, of her mind, of her body. Once she had been so strong. She'd gotten straight A's; she'd been a runner, capable of making her muscles do her will. But ever since the Life's Blood had awakened within her, she'd become another creature entirely. One whose needs, wants, wills, were secondary to her desires, her lusts, the demands of her body. All she could think about now was sex – of her hunger, of this need for satiation. It was like a drug...this addiction.

Can't you be stronger, Kal? Can't you just get over it?

She had to fight through this desire. She had to fight through this pleasure. She had to use her mind and not her body, to figure out what Nereti was up to, to stop her before more Carriers were slaughtered or drained dry by Nereti's vampire army. She had to work harder – to be *better*. She had to regain control over herself.

Still, she shuddered beneath Octavius' tongue, Nereti's body and her own fusing as one. Still, she screamed with delight when Octavius thrust into her, spreading apart her thighs and making her take all of him on. Still, she moaned his name over and over again.

And then one day, at last, she received an image – an image as clear as a photograph. Nereti and Octavius were lying in bed together – *she* and Octavius were lying in bed together – and they were talking idly of the plans they had for one another.

"The vampires are not all one," Nereti was sneering. "They have not yet all united under my banner. They are not in accord, with one mind. This troubles me."

"They will come, my Queen," Octavius murmured. "I swear it. They will come and worship you, just like before."

"But are you so sure?"

75

"I know that one day you will conquer all, my lovely Queen. I know that one day human and vampire alike will quake beneath your feet."

"But we still have enemies."

"Those that will not bend their knee and neck to us, we will smite," said Octavius, kissing her shoulder roughly, tracing the smooth skin with his light fingertips.

"But whom shall we smite next, my Consort, my love?"

"I have heard tell of one rebel tribe," Octavius' voice grew tight. "One tribe that will never swear allegiance to you. Stubborn insects, they are. Impudent ants. Deserving only of slaughter. Deserving to be stepped upon, pulverized, crushed and crumbled into dust."

"Where, my Consort?"

"They are in South Africa. They are strong – but they are too willful for their own good."

"There are many who have not yet bent the knee. Why them?"

"These are a stubborn kind. They will never

pledge allegiance to you – my spies have told me that much. Better to destroy them as soon as possible – to annihilate them as a warning to the others. Those who would defy you must see your wrath, so that they will know what is the fate of the betrayers and those who do not submit. They must know your power so that they might fear it, my lady Queen."

"Yes," Nereti was nodding slowly, taking pleasure, savoring the cruelty in his words. "Yes, my ruthless General, yes. We must send an army upon them, and if my power is as strong as I know it to be, they shall exist no more to blight the world with their betrayal. By tomorrow night, they shall be as nothing. And then the world will know how Nereti treats those who do not do her bidding. I am sure of it."

Octavius kissed her – deeply, richly. Kalina could feel his familiar taste – that taste of dark chocolate and hot chili pepper, of musky sweat and smoke. The taste that automatically made her mouth water in hunger. She tasted it and longed for his scent to linger upon her lips and tongue. She tasted it and desired him all the more, even as she felt her heart constrain and break within her chest. *How can he be kissing her so passionately, so fully? This can be no glamour. He believes it – all of it. He believes in her. He loves her. He loves her – not me...*

No, she could not give into this despair! She had to keep her eyes and ears open, to foretell the plan, to forestall this destruction...

"I should be able to send a few of our best fighting vampires out there," Octavius' voice was so cold, so untroubled in the face of death. "No need to send an entire army. If these rebel vampires are but few, as I know them to be, then we need not spare too many of our finest to eliminate them utterly."

Nereti nodded again. "Yes, yes," she cooed. "Good, good, my general. We must conserve the strength of all our vampires for the great battle, the one that is to come. These smaller missions, vital though they must be to consolidating our powers, must not require the expenditure of too many vampires."

"Agreed, my Queen." Octavius bowed down

low, so that his lips were level with her thighs. He kissed her there, nipping lightly at the copper-tanned flesh. "You are indeed a wise and intelligent Queen, and it honors me to serve you...in all ways, always."

Nereti ran her fingers through his long dark hair, twisting and pulling it between her tapered, slender fingers. She pulled him up to face her, fixing her intense gaze upon him, letting him see the pride and arrogance in her desire for him. "You understand me perfectly, my General," Nereti said. "Stay and lie with me. I command it. You must stay and lie here with me while we dispatch our vampires to the rebel tribe. There is no need for me to be deprived of the pleasure you give me, just to step upon these minor bugs. It is my wish that you remain here – that the services you *render* me be performed here. Your advisement pleases me greatly, my good General..."

Kalina could feel Octavius running his hands and tongue once more upon her skin, burying his mouth in her, giving himself up with utter conviction to the desire he felt for her, the overwhelming need that gave force and fire to all that he did. Yes, Octavius was overwhelmed with desire – and so was she, feeling the tingle of his flesh upon her own. Overwhelmed with desire...for another.

Kalina swallowed down her rage, her pain, her pleasure all at once. She forced herself out of the trace, coming to with a start, once more in her hotel room in Morocco, once more surrounded by silks and fine fabrics. Samson, Jaegar, Justin, and Max were sitting all around her.

"What did you see?" Justin asked urgently. "What did you discover? We heard you making these noises..."

Jaegar looked to the floor, clearly embarrassed.

"Uh, nothing..." Kalina could feel her face flush. "I mean...I'm fine. I heard Nereti's plan."

"What is it?" Max leaped over to Kalina's side. "What is it, honey?"

"There's a rebel vampire tribe in South Africa...Nereti says that they'll never bend the knee to her, so she wants them eliminated. She's sending

80

a small contingent over there – not her whole army. She says she wants to conserve as many men as possible for the "battle that is to come.""

"What battle?" Max furrowed her brow.

"She didn't say. She said that right now she's sending a small group of vampires – not Octavius – to pick off this tribe in South Africa. To send a message to the other vampires who don't want to submit to her: that she will never be defeated."

"We can't let that happen," Samson gritted his teeth. "Nereti's reputation is almost as important to her as her military power. If this tribe gets wiped out, who knows how many other rebel tribes will bend the knee in fear and cowardice?"

"We can't all be as noble as Octavius was," said Jaegar, and Kalina could detect a slight bitterness, a slight sarcasm in his voice. "They will bend. Or else they will break."

"Then we have to stop them!" Kalina's voice was stern, insistent. "We have to go to South Africa – now!"

"If neither Nereti or Octavius is going, they

shouldn't be too hard to pick off," said Samson roughly, and Kalina knew that he was hankering for revenge – after all, a horde of Nereti's foot soldiers had nearly seen him baked alive under the sun.

"Then it's time to fight," Kalina said resolutely. "It's time to go. We must not hold back."

"Very well," Jaegar assented. "That is our next step. We must head to South Africa in search of this tribe. And we must fly!"

Chapter 7

So they flew south, crossing the continent. Kalina felt her blood boil as she followed Jaegar across the wind, feeling the grains of sands whipping against her skin, as hard and lacerating as diamonds. It was almost painful, she thought, these rough breezes, but she welcomed the pain. Her body was in such a state of tension, such a coiled state of desire and need, that she felt as if even pain were some relief, however small, from the flooding intensity of her desire. How could she bear this? Kalina bit her lip and looked over to Jaegar, flying through the sky just ahead of her, hoping that neither Max, nor Samson, nor Justin would catch the gleam of desire in her eye. This feeling was overwhelming. She'd felt desire before, of course – desire so strong she hadn't been sure she could bear it. But this was something else entirely. This need was new. Kalina's longing for Jaegar, for Octavius, for *Stuart*, even, when she thought of Stuart, now living so peacefully in the Greystone Winery, was like bloodlust. Is this what vampires feel when they crave what they are forbidden to have?

This cursed desire to have that which will cause our fall?

Pull yourself together, Kalina, she snapped at herself. *Focus.* But how could she focus, when Jaegar's perfect muscles were rippling, glimmering in the dusky pink of twilight, catching every ray and refracting it back at her? How could she focus, when she looked at his dark lips, the colors of fresh rosebuds, and imagined him once more pressing those lips between her thighs, probing her inwardness, making her moan aloud with the sheer force of her need. She felt a shiver pass down her spine, trailing between her legs, as she thought of it.

Not even her fantasies had been able to sustain her. The experience of being inside Nereti's mind, of feeling Octavius deep within her, thrusting so powerfully she thought she would break open, had been a heady one. But if she had thought that it would be a way to expend this excess sexual energy, she was wrong. This desire was a thirst that could not be slaked, a drink that only increased the thirst with every tantalizing drop. No wonder why vampires are such sensual creatures.

"Funny," Kalina said softly as they flew over the deserts, watching the sands swirl beneath them. She leaned into Jaegar's ears. "Is this what bloodlust is like for you?"

"What do you mean?"

"This distraction. This hunger. This inability to do anything except think about...what you want?"

Jaegar grinned wickedly. "And what do you hunger for, my love? Not blood?"

"You know."

He laughed. "You're insatiable, Kal."

"*Is* it me?" Kalina's voice faltered as the memory of that other face came back to her, chilling her blood. "Or is it *her*? This aggression, this need for consummation, this control...it can't be good, can it?"

Blood Curse (Pulse #8)

"It certainly isn't bad for *me*!" Jaegar's smile was infectious.

"Before," Kalina said softly, "in my old life. I was always in control. I was always on top of everything. I never doubted that I could achieve whatever I want. I never doubted that my emotions were second to my will. But now I do. Now I know that no matter what I *will*, there's a part of me that is so close to losing control, every second. I'm not my own master, anymore. Or my own mistress."

"You could be *my* mistress."

"I just keep thinking...what happens if I can't control it? What happens if one day I completely give in, find myself unable to stop...that'll ruin everything, won't it? My status as a Carrier? My Life's Blood?"

"That won't happen." Jaegar furrowed his brow. "You're strong. We're both strong. And if you ever decide that one day I'm the vampire you want to turn, the vampire you want to change, your true love for the rest of our human lives....then we can give in together. But until then, I know you won't. You're stronger than you think you are. You're stronger than you give yourself credit for. But deep down, Kalina, my love. I see the real you. I see the you that you don't always see – when you're so busy being hard on yourself."

They began to see the deserts recede in the distance, giving way to new terrain: cities, townships, new formations in the sands.

"We're getting closer," Samson said. "I can smell it." He nodded. "These vampires are strong. Rebellious. They're the good guys. We need to protect them."

Max nodded. "It isn't easy for vampire communities to stand up to Nereti. Many have fallen already – reduced by cowardice to her puppets. But not these guys."

A series of caves appeared before them in the distance, shimmering with the night air. Moonlight flooded the view before them, like white milk poured out across the whole landscape.

"It's beautiful..." Kalina whispered.

"We must keep them safe," Max said again.

"We owe it to them. To all the vampires left who follow the Consortium. Who fight the good fight."

"Let's go," said Samson.

"Who goes there?" A warrior vampire stepped forward, his dark skin gleaming in the moonlight. He took another step forward, sizing them up. "Samson?"

"My friend!" Samson embraced him quickly. "My dear Uzo. We have come to warn you. You are in grave danger. Nereti's men march on you tonight – they'll be here any minute."

The vampire's brow furrowed, but he betrayed no fear. "I knew she would come to seek vengeance," he said. "I did not know the hour. I am not afraid to die for my cause, if I must."

"You need not perish!" Samson said.

"They have Carrier blood with them."

Kalina smiled. "*We* have Carrier blood, too."

The vampire looked her up and down. "You mean...?"

"A Carrier," said Samson. "And what's more, she is one who knows the secret of how to defeat those vampires with Life's Blood in their veins."

"Look!" Justin opened his backpack to reveal fifty or more stakes, newly sharpened, rubies set into the wood. They shone with a blood-red vengeance.

"This kills them," Kalina's voice was harsh and firm. "Let them try to stop us now."

"I have heard tell of such an antidote..." The vampire took the stake in his hands, fingering it with reverence. "But never until now have I believed it existed. I thought it was merely a fairy tale, designed to console those of us about to turn to ash that perhaps one day there would be others who could fight back against those who would seek to oppress us."

"No longer," said Kalina. "We can fight back. We can win."

"They expect it to be a surprise attack," Jaegar said, "which means we have the advantage."

"The caves," Uzo said, a grin spreading across his face. His teeth shone bright white in the moonlight. "They are a vast labyrinth. We know the way. Our enemies do not. If we hide outside them, our enemies will come looking for us in the caves, expecting to slaughter us while we slumber. Once they are safely inside, we can surround them and re-enter."

"I like the way you think, old friend," said Samson. "You see, Uzo is an old ally of mine."

"I saved his life plenty of times in the old days," Uzo's laugh was deep and throaty. "So perhaps it is good that now you will save mine. We are even today, old friend."

"Not so," Samson said, putting his hand to his chest. "For if I recall rightly, you saved my life at least three times."

"Let us hope you will not have occasion to need to rescue me two more," said Uzo, and with that they set about to subvert the ambush. The vampires moved swiftly, leaving the cave network and hiding in the brush and stone that surrounded them.

Then, they had only to wait. Kalina felt her heart pounding and tried to swallow down her fear. Even with the element of surprise, Nereti's men were not the most welcome bunch. Could they hear the drum-beat of her terrified heart, she wondered, hoping she had been able to keep her pulse quiet from their ears.

"Shh!" Jaegar whispered into her ear. "They're coming."

And come they did. Fifty vampires were marching towards them.

"I recognize the one at the front," whispered Samson. "That's Perseus. One of Nereti's most devoted followers. Once her great General, though I think from that particular position he has been deposed..."

Kalina winced as images of Octavius and Nereti intertwined flashed through her brain.

She could see Perseus in the distance – the familiar crazed eyes that signified Life's Blood coursing through the veins. She shuddered at the sight of him, shuddered thinking about what young Life's Blood Carriers had been slaughtered to get that blood down his throat. He had been handsome once, she could see that much, but evil had transformed his features, casting his whole expression and

91

countenance in a waxwork model of cruelty. Was this what Octavius too would one day become? Kalina shuddered at the thought. Would her beloved Octavius turn this fierce, this ferocious, this insane, under Nereti's noxious influence?

But she couldn't think about that now. There was no time for wondering or for recriminations. She had to focus on one thing and one thing only – saving Uzo and his men.

"It's working," hissed Uzo in her ear as the vampires made their way into the caves, their footsteps virtually silent upon the soft desert sands.

"Those fools are asleep in the darkness yet," sneered Perseus as he passed by, just over Kalina's head. "We shall slaughter them, each and every one, and we shall at last find that which we seek."

That which we seek? Kalina furrowed her brow. *Isn't this supposed to be putting down a rebellion? What are they looking for?*

"If we can get a fresh taste of the Carrier, too!" one of Perseus's underlings licked his lips, showing gleaming fangs.

"Nay!" Perseus rounded on his underling with a horrific growl. "You know Nereti's orders. She wants the Carrier alive."

"All the better...I know ways to torture that don't leave marks."

"No!" Perseus said. "You know the orders. Nereti wants to do all the torturing herself."

Kalina felt her stomach lurch as Perseus and his men vanished inside the cave.

"They're all in," Jaegar said.

"Very well," Uzo brandished his stake. "Now it is time for attack."

And with that, they rounded on Nereti's men, following them into the caves, tiptoeing up behind them and goring them straight through with ruby stakes.

The first round was the easiest. Caught unaware in the midst of their stealth attack, the vampires dropped to the floor and vanished into ash so silently that their compatriots did not even hear them. It was not until Kalina and her allies had each killed two or three vampires that the others began to notice what was going on.

By then it was too late. Uzo and his vampires would have been formidable enough on their own, Kalina guessed, but with ruby stakes between their fingers they were unstoppable.

Soon, they had slaughtered each and every one of the invaders.

Chapter 8

"We did it!" Jaegar turned to Kalina, joy in his glimmering eyes. The ash of the vanquished vampires was floating in the air all around them, shining in the first light of dawn. "Kalina, you were amazing." He took her in his arms, holding her tight, kissing her softly. "I'm so proud of you."

Kalina stood for a while, staring at the stake in her hands. Her heart was beating louder than ever now; it felt like thunder breaking through the morning sky. She'd killed vampires before, she knew, hundreds of them by now. But something felt different this time. The act of killing had boiled her blood in a new way. She felt happy, tired, but more than that, she felt a strange rush of adrenaline coursing through her, a strange joy. As if...she had *enjoyed* it. Enjoyed the killing, not merely as something that needed to be done, for the common good but as something in its own right, an act of

95

power, an act of vanquishing, that gave her a bizarre kind of strength.

Kalina shivered. Could Nereti's influence be stronger even than she thought? Strong enough for her to *enjoy* slaughter?

"No," she said aloud. "No – that can't be."

"What is it, Kal?" Jaegar rushed to her side.

"It...feels good, doesn't it?" Kalina swallowed hard. "Killing."

"Sometimes," Jaegar admitted. A shadow flitted across his face, and Kalina knew that he was thinking of all the innocents he had killed, back in the old days, back in his days of evil. "Sometimes it felt *too* good."

"I can't stop shaking..." Kalina said. "It's...invigorating..."

"No," Uzo took a step forward. "No, it must not be that way. Not for a true warrior."

Samson nodded. "Human, vampire alike – I must learn to despise what I do. For only when I look upon the true horror of death can I kill with honor. Octavius taught me that."

Octavius! Kalina felt another pang, a strong one, at the mention of his name. Had he really been the one to wreak such devastation on the caves? Had he really been the one to send Nereti's forces to this South African tribe?

Octavius!

No sooner had she thought the name than she saw him once again in her mind's eye – a vision so strong that it blocked out her human eyes and left her blind and reeling. Before her was Octavius, naked and glistening, his stomach taut, his muscles chiseled, his expression full of darkness and rage. And rage, too, seemed to course through her, an infernal and primal anger that manifested itself in a wailing, furious scream that almost deafened her.

"No!" Nereti was shouting. "No!" It was the scream of a queen whose will had never once been defied, whose demands had never once been question. A scream of ancient, evil power mingled with the all too human note of disbelief.

"How can this be?" Nercti was shouting at Octavius. "Who was it that betrayed us? Surely they must have had advance notice – that is the only excuse for this travesty. One among us is a betrayer. I will find him. I will torture him. I will slaughter him. I will *destroy him utterly.*"

"We shall torture him for centuries, my Queen," Octavius promised, kissing Nereti deeply and roughly. Kalina moaned slightly at the sweet, tantalizing taste of him. "He has led to the deaths of many of your finest soldiers."

"Do you think I care about my warriors? Carrion, they are. Mere machines, fit only for death – theirs or those of another. No, it is the diamonds I care for! We needed those diamonds..."

Immediately Kalina remembered what Perseus had said. *We will find them.* What was it that they were looking for? What were these diamonds?

"Diamonds," she said aloud, flashing back to her surroundings. Uzo and Jaegar were standing over her, looking worried.

"Kalina, what happened?" Jaegar took her hand.

"What are these diamonds that Nereti was

looking for?" Kalina asked Uzo. "Why did she want them?"

Uzo sighed heavily. "We have been keeping that secret for many centuries," he said. "We are the guardians of something very precious indeed. Nereti's raid was not only about defiance. We also had something she wanted badly. Very badly."

"What's so special about these diamonds?" Kalina asked.

Uzo took a step forward, looking around at the others, hesitating. "I must tell you all," he said. He barked orders at his men, demanding that they begin the work of cleaning up the mess. "I must tell you in private," he said.

He led Kalina deep into the caves, deep into their darkest hidden heart. He produced a key from around his neck and unlocked a carved wooden door, intricately decorated with some of the finest woodwork Kalina had ever seen. Once they were safely inside, he locked the door once more behind them.

Kalina gasped. All around her were the most

beautiful jewels she'd ever seen. Each crystal, each glimmering diamond, shone with the light of a thousand moons, catching the glow of the candles all around them. In each she could see reflected her own face.

"These diamonds," Uzo said to her, "are no ordinary diamonds. They are powerful. They can destroy the most powerful, the most ancient of any vampires. Or at least, they will be, in the hands of the right person. These diamonds are in fact the strongest substance that exists, or ever has existed on earth. When wielded by the one who has been prophesied, they can be used to defeat whole armies. We could not harness their power before. But now we can. Nereti believes she is the one fated to use these diamonds. But now, as I look at you, I am more sure than ever that she is wrong."

He took out one of the diamonds and placed it in Kalina's palm. Immediately it began glowing bright, dark red.

"Light and life defeat the bringer of death and destruction," said Uzo. "You look just like her, you know. But whereas her heart is black, yours is full of the sun. There must be a reason that you two are so similar – a connection."

"No connection!" Kalina cried.

"You are opposites, linked by what divides you. Light and dark, life and death, are bound together always. You bear her image, yet you have goodness within you, the human and the vampire together, vampire speed and strength and a human heart, capable of the greatest love. The most bountiful love. I see from your face you have loved much."

Kalina flushed. "Yes," she said.

"I believe you are the one who is prophesied to use these," Uzo said. "These are the diamonds that are your bounty. When the time comes to use them, you will know what to do."

Immediately another flash came over Kalina, another series of images flitting across her brain. The rage came once more, stronger this time, overwhelming, even.

"We must send another trope out there," cried

Nereti, her voice terrible in its anger. "We must get our hands on these diamonds. We cannot allow them to keep them. We cannot allow our enemies to reach them. Take all the vampires you can spare, we must go immediately."

"But my darling, you said this was only a minor raid," Octavius kissed Nereti, tracing his lips along her naked shoulders, her naked back. "Why do you wish to spend all your energy on this minor tribe?"

"Defiance must be punished!" cried Nereti. "And besides, it pleases me to take their bounty. These diamonds – I shall wear them, and then the whole world will know what happens to those who cross me."

"We can get diamonds anywhere, my love," Octavius said.

"These diamonds will be stained with the blood of my enemies," Nereti replied, "and they will be all the more beautiful for it. I will have these and none others to wear in my crown."

Why was Nereti hiding the secret of the

102

diamonds from Octavius? Kalina couldn't help but wonder. Did she not trust Octavius fully, even now? Why keep secrets from her beloved General?

Then, with a jolt, Kalina heard another voice – Nereti's voice. The inward workings of her mind – sounding as cold and cruel as the hissing of a snake before it strikes.

Do not reveal all, yet. You are a Queen. You must trust no one, not even the man, not even he who makes you moan. He is your slave, not your equal. He must not know. Nobody can know your weakness. They must see you only as a Queen, unassailable. When first these diamonds were used to create the First Carrier, the potion that first boiled the Life's Blood in the veins of a young woman for the first time, their purity and strength were unknown. Only a few know the source of Life's Blood – only a few know that it is your weakness. You must destroy them all so that the secret never gets out.

Get the diamonds – bury the secret – increase your strength, hide your weakness. Then you shall be truly immortal – free of fear, free of care. Then you will

103

reign over all the world.

Your power is not enough. There is no such thing as enough power. There is no such thing as enough strength. The hunger of evil is never-ending. The thirst of evil is never-quenched. There is no such thing as enough. You must be stronger, better, faster, more powerful, always...

"Octavius," now Nereti was speaking aloud, in a voice far sweeter, in honeyed tones that set Kalina's teeth on edge. "How naïve you are sometimes when it comes to the workings of pure evil. You are fortunate to be so blind. I enjoy you. I enjoy your body very much. Perhaps it is because of the blood I am drunk with, the blood I drained from the Carrier, who was bonded with you once, that I feel such pleasure in your tongue, in all your parts. But you are still so innocent, so pure, so...human, almost. In time you will understand. In time you will grow harder against any emotions you may have. You will be a great General once more, and you will understand what it means to wear the blood of one's enemies upon the diamonds in one's crown."

"Yes, my Queen," Octavius bowed his head. "We will send out more vampires to find these diamonds, as you wish. All of them, if you wish it."

"I cannot abide incompetence," snarled Nereti. "No more underlings. We will go ourselves to lead this battle."

She eyed Octavius, taking him in before pulling him in for a deep kiss. She licked his bare chest, savoring each morsel of flesh, before sinking her teeth into it, drinking from his blood before licking shut the wound. "You taste delicious, General," she said. "And you taste like a vampire fully under my command. For an instant perhaps I wondered if you were my betrayer. But your taste is pure evil. Good." She kissed him on the lips. "It would be such a pity to have to destroy you, General."

Octavius did not flinch. "I will prepare our men," he said. "The battle ahead shall be our triumph."

Chapter 9

Kalina was exhausted. She'd never known such exhaustion before. Her bones ached. Her blood was tired, as if the very act of coursing through her veins was an overwhelming one. She felt every nerve ending in her body shudder with the pain of holding herself together. What was happening to her? She'd fought battles before – battles far harder than this one – and won. But now she was tired, bone-tired. She needed to rest.

"It's the visions," Jaegar said, putting his hand on her shoulder. "I know how they are. Even when I have visions of you, sometimes, it tires me out. All that psychic energy. But to get inside the head of a person you hate...I can only imagine what it's doing to you."

What it's doing to me, Kalina thought mournfully. At once tantalizing her, offering her the greatest pleasures, those she had for so long been denied, and simultaneously destroying her, breaking her heart over and over again. And she felt, too, the effects of that evil, Nereti's darkness, seeping into her, like an ink spill into her heart. Nereti's darkness was whetting her lusts, her appetites, making her colder and crueler, making her revel in Jaegar's submission to her in a way she had never done before. Nereti was like her dark twin – her other self – "two sides of the same coin," Uzo had said. A shadow that she could never fully be free from. She swallowed hard.

"Tomorrow," she said, "we bring the fight to them. We don't wait for them to strike twice. We go straight to the palace where Octavius is being kept – we slay every last vampire, we fix Octavius, restore his brain..."

"Kalina," Jaegar's voice was low and full of pity. "Even if we defeat Nereti, there's no guarantee that it will fix Octavius. There's no evidence that he'll automatically go back to the way he was."

She shut out his words. "He will," it was all

she could think to say. "I know him. He will."

"In which case," Samson said. "Let the humans get some rest. Max and Kal should go to a hotel – rest for a couple of hours, get your strength up for the next attack." He had not flinched. The idea of an attack on Nereti, of an attack that would certainly threaten all their lives, seemed to mean nothing to him now. He had fought too many battles to really know fear.

The vampires flew the humans into town. "The Marriot Johannesburg should suit," Jaegar grinned," at Kalina. "I put my card down – got us the presidential suite..."

Samson cleared his throat. "As for us...we vampires need to feed." He looked around at Justin and Jaegar.

Jaegar took a step forward, clasping Kalina's hand in his. "I can feed all I want right here," he said. "I'll stay with you, Kal. Keep you safe."

"Don't be foolish," Samson rolled his eyes. "If you haven't fed you're not at peak strength, and then we'd all suffer for it. Do what I have commanded, my boy, and get yourself some fresh blood, if you cannot find vampire wine. Just be...careful with your appetites. Show the young one..." he motioned at Justin. "How to find a willing victim, how to feed without draining."

"I know all that already!" Justin cut in, a bit too eagerly.

"He's still so young," Samson added.

Jaegar nodded. "You're right," he said, taking Justin's hand. "We'll be back soon!" And with that, the two of them flew off, Samson close behind them, leaving Max and Kalina alone.

They made their way to the suite. Certainly Jaegar's sort of place, Kalina thought grimly. Silks and satins everywhere – gorgeously decorated in a splendor that she still hadn't gotten used to, even after more than a few years with the Greystones and their maker. Still, she could certainly more than get used to the food. Room service brought up dish after dish – meat, fish, vegetable alike – and Kalina and Max wolfed them down, unable even to speak in their hunger.

109

"Tomorrow we fight, I guess," Kalina said to Max. "Do you think we can win?"

"No," Max's voice was soft and almost bitter. "But we fight anyway. That's what this battle is about. That's what we always do. We won't win by numbers alone, Kal. But we have smarts, and strategy – things most vampires don't have. And we're on the side of good. Deep down, I really believe that makes a difference." She swallowed. "It has to."

"Mom?"

"Yes?"

"What's happening to me?"

"What do you mean?"

"Nereti – Nereti's influence. Sometimes it feels like she's taking over, like she has too much power over me...it makes me scared..."

"Oh, Kalina..." Max put an arm around Kalina's shoulder. "We all have that, you know. All of us, Carriers. A potential for darkness, for destruction, that could obliterate all that we've worked for. But I trust you, my dear. I trust you to overcome it. Generations of Life's Blood Carriers have wrestled with this darkness, and many – most – have won. I knew, sooner or later, you would come to the darkness. Perhaps I should have warned you. I did not want to frighten you. But now..."

She was cut off by the whooshing sound of flight. Jaegar had bolted back into the room, collapsing in a heap of exhaustion on the floor.

"What is it?" Kalina tensed.

"The mines...the vampires at the mines..." Jaegar was in shock. "They've slaughtered them all?"

"*How*?" Kalina gaped. It hadn't been more than an hour – there was no way a vampire army could get there in time.

"Uzo, everybody. Samson had left his sword at the mines for them to enhance with the diamond powder – we went to pick it back up once we'd fed, and found the mines desecrated, the vampires all dust..."

"An army can't move that fast..."

"*Nereti could...*" Samson said darkly. "We were fools to miss it. She didn't send an army, after all. She went herself. She can appear faster than

111

ordinary vampires. And her fury may have only boosted her powers. I have no doubt that this destruction is her handiwork."

"The place looked like it had been ransacked," Jaegar furrowed his brow with concern. "They were looking for something, that's for sure."

"I just hope she didn't find it," Samson said. "The last thing we need is for Nereti to achieve another one of her despicable ends."

"I...don't think she did." Kalina looked up slowly, taking from around her neck the pouch of diamonds Uzo had given her. "They gave them to me for safekeeping. Whatever Nereti found at the mines, it wasn't what she wanted. They're her weakness – like rubies, but stronger still."

Before anyone else had a chance to react, Jaegar was upon her, grasping the pouch from around her neck so violently that she choked on the string. "Give this to me," he said.

"Ow, Jaegar, stop, you're hurting me!"

The string broke and Jaegar stood with the pouch in his hands. He began undoing the pouch,

112

about to open them...

"What is it, Jaegar?"

His voice was high and cold and nothing like that of the Jaegar she knew. "Stay away, human!"

"Jaegar?" Had he fed on Life's Blood by mistake? "What's gotten into you?"

"This belongs to me," he hissed.

"What? Why?"

"Because," Samson stood in the window, sniffing the air, Justin close behind him. "This isn't Jaegar."

"Glamour?" Max looked worried. Only very powerful vampires could glamour as other vampires.

"Who are you, then?" Kalina focused her power, all of her Life's Blood strength, through her eyes. The beautiful form of Jaegar began to glimmer and shine before her, fading slightly, so that beneath his face she could see that of another – perhaps a rare survivor from the mine attack, a spy...

"What do you want, Soldier?"

The spy looked surprised that she could see through him.

"I told you, give those diamonds back to me, spy!"

"You should speak to me with more respect! I'm about to become the most powerful vampire in the world. All I have to do is gulp these down and then I'll be more powerful than you, than Nereti, than *any* of you. And worlds will quake and shake before *me*."

What? Kalina had heard that these diamonds were a weapon, but nothing about them enhancing anyone's power...

"Now, bow down and fear..."

It was too late. Samson had rushed him from behind, knocking him to the floor, sending the pouch into the air and the diamonds flying in all directions, sparkling and glimmering with a strange red light.

"No!" The vampire leaped forward, grabbing a single diamond in his fist. Then he began to scream.

It was the most disturbing, most terrible sound Kalina had ever heard. The sound of agony – the smell of burning vampire flesh.

Immediately Samson grabbed another of the

diamonds through the pouch, and pressed it against the vampire's skin.

He screamed louder, his pain greater, as the burning spread across his skin. It took him a full ten minutes to die.

Kalina had to close her eyes and walk away to withstand the sound, the smell, the screaming. Nobody should have to suffer like that, she thought, not even one of Nereti's men. She walked from the suite living room into the bedroom, sitting on the bed and closing her eyes.

Those who defy me shall all die.

It was Nereti's voice, as cold and distorted as ever. Another vision? Kalina steeled her body to enter Nereti's mind once again.

This isn't a vision, girl.

And then Kalina realized it. The voice was coming from straight behind her.

She whirled around to face her – those same eyes, that same nose, that same horrifically malignant smile.

Their eyes connected

Blood Curse (Pulse #8)

"It's high time we met again, Kalina," hissed Nereti. "And this time you won't make it past the door to escape."

Chapter 10

Kalina felt like a mouse, transfixed by the eyes of a snake. Terror pounded through her, her heart ricocheting off her chest, her breath frozen within her lungs, weighing them down. She had never been this close to Nereti in her full power and glory before. Her presence was overwhelming. The feeling of her, so near, was the feeling of pure evil. It lapped at her like the waves of an ocean. It consumed her entirely. Was this the very core of darkness – was this what it was like, to come face to face with the worst that vampiredom had to offer? Kalina wanted to run, wanted to scream, but instead her mind went blank. The enormity of Nereti's cruelty floored her. She saw visions in her mind's eye, flickering past her in black and white – like old film footage – visions of all that Nereti had done: of murders she had order or committed, rape and pillage that had been carried out by her command, centuries of horror wrought upon the innocent and the guilty alike.

And Kalina felt all of it. Her head was throbbing, aching, splitting like it was about to burst open like an overripe fruit; her heart was beating faster and faster; her whole body was in agony. The telepathic connection that had linked her to Nereti was stronger than ever now, flooding through her entire being. She could see, hear, feel, smell, taste all the evil that Nereti had ever wrought upon the world.

No, Kalina, she whispered to herself, her breath shallow, her heart faster than ever, *you need to beat this. You need to stay calm. Focus. Focus.*

But how could she focus? She could think of nothing but the faces of the dead, appearing one by one in so many multitudes before her; she could think of nothing but the pain that each one of them – men, women, and children – must have felt before dying by Nereti's hand.

She had encountered evil before. She had stared down Mal, down so many vampires who had done terrible things, and she had done so clear-eyed, without fear. This was different. Looking at Nereti was like looking into a dark mirror of her soul: a version of herself that had chosen darkness instead of light, that had embraced the darkness, that threatened to consume her entirely.

"Well, little girl?" Nereti's tongue slithered between her lips. "Not quite so brave now, are we? Not when you are faced with your Queen. Bow down, girl, before you die – perhaps it will buy you a second or two of life before I watch it slip so slowly out of your eyes. Bow down to your Queen, to your mistress, to she who commands you to die!"

The words jolted Kalina back into life. Rage – pure, defensive anger – swept over her. *How dare she?* Kalina thought. *How dare she speak to me this way? How dare she try to make me her slave?* Defiance bubbled up like molten lava within her. Immediately her muscles tensed; her body and jaw hardened; her fear calcified and transformed into strength.

No, Kalina thought. She would not be broken. She would not be beaten. She would not let this evil consume her. She would be strong – she would fight. She might die in the attempt, but she knew it was better to die fighting, than die on her knees like a miserable little coward. Nothing – not even Nereti – would make her sacrifice her dignity.

"Come on, girl..." Nereti's voice was sickeningly lilting. "Give me the diamonds, little girl, and gain a few seconds more of that precious little mediocrity you call life."

"No!" The force of the words shook her. They sounded like they came from a stranger's lips, in a stranger's voice – hollow and echoing from a million miles away. "Never."

In an instant Kalina came to life. She could feel the blood boiling in her veins – the Life's Blood, defiant and strong; it seemed to know what to do even before the knowledge reached her consciousness. As quick as lightning, she was reaching inside the bag of diamonds, rushing towards Nereti, the sharp edge of the diamond glinting in the evening light.

A voice seemed to echo inside her brain. *You*

must defeat Nereti. You must kill her. You are the chosen one. This is how you survive.

It was the voice of the Life's Blood – delphic and oracular – an ancient power that seemed to call to her, to control her, to make her its own. Kalina succumbed to its call.

But Nereti was quicker still. In a flash, she had dodged Kalina's attack, gliding smoothly to the other end of the room.

"What's so special about these diamonds, huh?" The Life's Blood had made her bold, now; it had cast out all her fear. She was defiant; she was consumed by the adrenaline that coursed through her. "Why do you want them so badly?"

"It is not for you to question me, little girl," Nereti sneered. "I am your Queen; you are only a puny mortal before me."

"I'm just saying." Kalina put her hands on her hips. "You're going to an awful lot of trouble for these diamonds."

"All precious metals and gems of the earth belong to me!" snapped Nereti. "They are my dominion. The whole world is my dominion, now, and this is my prize. All those who defy me shall perish..."

"Are you so sure about that?" Kalina asked.

She struck again, slicing at Nereti with the diamond, listening for the high whistling sound of the gemstone cutting through the empty air.

But Nereti dodged her again – appearing and disappearing as she moved, faster than light itself, from corner to corner of the room.

At last Kalina sliced one final, desperate time, putting all her strength into the action.

It was a mistake.

She had misjudged her target; she had lunged too quickly; she lost control of her balance and stumbled, letting the diamond fall to the floor.

In an instant both Nereti and Kalina were rushing for the diamond.

But something stopped them – a force of light that flashed gold and sent them both reeling backwards.

"What the..."

The light from the window was streaming onto the diamond. But the refracted light was pouring onto the side of the wall, reflecting an image there, like a picture in a projector slide. It was a map – a map of Egypt Kalina realized – a map of a desert and a series of caves, labyrinthine like the combs of a beehive, each one leading into the last. The layout looked uncannily familiar.

I must get the rest of the diamonds to show me where...

Kalina's head snapped up. For a moment, she thought Nereti had been speaking aloud. But Nereti's beautiful face remained unmoving, implacable. Her lips had not parted.

With surprise, Kalina realized what she had heard. Here, in this proximity, she was privy to Nereti's inner thoughts. She could hear inside Nereti's mind, as surely as if it had been her own. But Nereti showed no sign of realizing this. Her gaze was fixed on Kalina with hideous hatred in her eyes.

More images appeared, unbidden, in Kalina's mind – images from Nereti. She saw the cave in her mind's eye, and with a shock realized where it was. It was the cave where the ancient vampires, slaughtered on Octavius' watch, had all been on their guard. But surely Nereti's vampires had already searched the cave thoroughly – why would they have been unable to find what they sought....

No...no...

"Unfortunately..." Now Nereti was turning to her, her fanged teeth glinting in the light of the evening. Her voice was silky smooth. "I don't have any time to waste on killing you at the moment. I have bigger plans, far bigger plans, that don't allow me to waste my time fighting a puny mortal like you. I'll have to let someone else finish you off." She let loose a cackle that chilled Kalina's bones.

With that, Nereti flew from the room, leaving Kalina in shock.

What had happened to make Nereti flee so suddenly? What did she want? Where was she going?

Kalina was tempted to run – to make her way back to Jaegar and Justin, to Max and Samson and safety. But a terrible curiosity was burning in her breast. If she let Nereti get away now, she'd never know the reason for her mysterious exit – and she'd never know what it was Nereti was after. What was it about those caves – reflected in the diamond – that held the secret: to ultimate power, or ultimate destruction she did not know.

She had to make a choice. Safety – or another brush with darkness?

Her blood prickled within her veins, and she knew that her choice was already made. It was a match to the death with them now. She would pursue Nereti until one of them was destroyed – there was no other way out. The two of them were linked, now. By blood, by hatred, by the ancient power that bound them as one.

She flew swiftly from the window, hot on Nereti's heels. Her heart was pounding so loudly within her chest that it sounded like thunder. In the distance, she could see Nereti, getting smaller and smaller on the horizon; her muscles burned as she forced herself to fly faster and faster towards that shimmering dot.

Blood Curse (Pulse #8)

Jaegar, Justin, Max, Samson...

She sent telepathic messages to everyone she could think of, trying to let them know where she was, where she was going. They had to follow her, now – wherever they were – she hoped they got the message. There was no time to find them and tell them where she was going. She had to pursue Nereti, now, or lose the chance forever.

"You bitch..." Kalina whispered under her breath.

The rage that she felt was overwhelming, all-consuming, as powerful as her lust had been. All at once she wanted nothing more than to kill Nereti – as slowly and as cruelly as Nereti had killed so many others – to make her suffer, to make her write in agony, to make her scream as loudly as her victims had screamed.

She cared for nothing, now, but vengeance. Vengeance for Octavius. Vengeance for all those who had died and been tortured in her name.

Nereti may be evil – but she had not counted on Kalina's will being as iron, as implacable as her

126

own. Kalina would make her suffer the same fate her victims had suffered. Kalina would make her sink to her knees. Kalina would make her bow down before her.

She whispered like one possessed, in a voice that was not her own. "Just you wait, Nereti. You'll see who's Queen now..."

Chapter 11

What was happening to her? As she flew through the air, the breeze slicing like a knife against her alabaster skin, Kalina tried to make sense of the feelings, the thoughts, the raging emotions that were coming down like a thunderstorm into her brain. She had never felt like this before. She'd feared her enemies – she'd longed to defeat them – she had felt such abject horror and abhorrence for Mal and his men. But such hatred – such intense, ferocious desire to cause pain – this was new to her. This she had never experienced before. When she thought of Nereti, she thought only of her own anger: her own desire to have her revenge. She didn't just want to defeat Nereti. No – worse – she wanted to make her *suffer*. She wanted to make her feel pain.

Kalina swallowed, feeling a shiver run up and down her spine. What was making her feel this way? These emotions – like the lust that had just a few

128

hours earlier prompted her to savagely throw herself at Jaegar – weren't normal, weren't *hers*. They seemed to come from an outside force: a kind of dark possession she could neither understand nor control.

Was this Nereti's plan? The thought made her throat dry up with horror. Ever since Nereti's thoughts had begun to meld with her own, ever since the telepathy had started to bind them, ever since she had been able to dream of Octavius' body twined in hers, and feel the palpable power of his skin against her own, she had been – not quite herself. Her soul had been invaded by another, the evil seeping into her like spilled ink. Was this Nereti's presence, in her, making her feel this way? Was this hatred, this anger, just another way that Nereti was getting under her skin, getting that much closer to defeating her?

"No..." Kalina whispered under her breath. "No, it can't be."

She couldn't let Nereti win. Not like this. She couldn't let this anger, this hatred overtake her, make her start to question her own judgment, her own decisions, even her own sanity. She couldn't let her...

You can't let her escape.

The voice in her head was louder now.

You can't let her get away. You must find her – find – chase – kill. It was her own voice, magnified and distorted, as if coming from a million miles away. *You must defeat her.*

"No..." Kalina breathed again. She had to fight this force, this power that was overtaking her. She had to keep a cool head, keep control over the thoughts that threatened to lead her down the path of darkness.

A sharp whizzing through the air interrupted her thoughts as she flew. All her muscles tensed at once – coiled like those of a panther, ready to spring. Someone was following her.

She turned only slightly, but her vampire eyes took in all that she needed to see, her peripheral vision sharper than it had ever been. Five of Nereti's vampire generals were following after her, hot upon her heels.

"Damn..." she muttered, and sped up. She was barely able to keep up with Nereti, even as she flew as fast as she could; her heart ricocheted within her chest; she dodged and feinted her vampire pursuers as best she could.

Nereti meant business. For whatever reason, she didn't want to kill Kalina herself, but that was hardly a reprieve. Taking on four or five vampire assassins was one thing when she was with the others. But fighting one to five would be no easy matter. Her best chance was to outstrip them, to deal with Nereti directly. If she could only take Nereti down, if she could only slay her – with the diamonds, perhaps – she knew the rest of the vampires would immediately bow down before her. They were like sheep, she thought – for all their purported fearsomeness – they cared only about following a strong leader, whoever that was.

Kalina looked around for any sign of the others – Jaegar, Justin, Samson, Max – anyone who could help her. But nobody was to be found.

They must not have gotten the message. Or

131

else they were otherwise engaged – fighting off more of Nereti's men. Kalina shuddered to think of the danger they might be in. But she couldn't focus on that now. She had to follow Nereti to the caves – had to find the source of the mystery, of Nereti's enigmatic obsession...

The words Uzo had spoken to her echoed in her ears. *You are the chosen one. You one the one destined to bring Nereti down.* This was where she was meant to be. Succeed or fail, live or die, this was what she had to do. This was the destiny she was promised to fulfill. There was not enough room in the whole world for the two of them. One of them had to die.

Kalina gritted her teeth and hoped that it would not be her.

At last the caves appeared in the distance, glimmering in the horizon of early dawn. They had been running all night – flying through the desert sky – and Kalina's muscles burned with exhaustion. She hoped Nereti too was fading, her energy flagging just as hers was – that it might, at least, be a fair fight.

But Nereti showed no signs of slowing down. As she entered the caves, slipping as quickly like a lightning bolt into the labyrinthine web beneath the earth's surface, she was as agile as ever.

Kalina would have to take her anyway.

She just hoped her Life's Blood was up to the task.

Kalina landed with a start, reeling as her feet touched the earth once more. There was no time to rest. She had to hit the ground running. Immediately she raced into the caves, following Nereti's scent, trying to use the force of the Life's Blood to sense where she had gone.

They were the same caves she had been in earlier. But something was different this time, Kalina noticed, with a sudden jolt. Something had changed. To her eyes, her ears, her nose, everything was the same. The place looked no different. But her blood was prickling, boiling, burning; her veins felt like they were on fire. A sudden pull – so strong she had no choice but to submit to it – overwhelmed her body, her mind, her soul. She felt as if she were an

133

animal that had been snared, that was now being drawn in, closer and closer, to the hunter who had caught her out...

She found herself in a large cavern, deep within the belly of the caves. The room was enormous, hexagonal in shape, lit only by a few candles scattered in candelabras about the room. Nereti stood in the center of the room, a cruel and mocking smile upon her porcelain white face, the ruby lips curved like a scimitar. In Nereti's hand was the one diamond she had taken from Kalina. Slowly, deliberately, she took the diamond and pressed it into the ground.

What was she doing? Kalina craned her neck to see. But no sooner had she taken in Nereti's action than the whole cavern began to shake. The diamond was trembling in the earth, causing a shudder to spread throughout the whole cave network, cracks splintering in the floor, along the walls, separating the ground. A deep chasm appeared, as if from the bowels of the earth, cleaving the room in two.

Kalina gasped as she looked down into the chasm. It seemed to have no end. Darkness followed upon darkness – an eternal abyss.

"So, this is what it's all about?" Kalina's words were quiet, so quiet that she didn't think Nereti had heard her. But as soon as the words were uttered, Nereti looked up and saw Kalina, a burning look of fury upon her austerely beautiful face. Surprise spread across her features. "How dare you follow me here?" she bellowed, her words echoing off the cavern walls. "How dare you try to usurp me? This is mine to have, not yours, imposter!" Her words hissed – they were terrible. "Just because you look like me does not mean you will be the one to inherit its power!"

Overcome by anger, Nereti stamped her foot. But the force was too great. Immediately, the whole cavern seemed to tremble and shake, the fault lines becoming more and more numerous, until the whole cave network had started to crumble.

"Kal, no!" a voice cried.

Kalina turned to see Jaegar and the others –

horror and confusion on their faces. But they had come a second too late. No sooner had she spied them than a huge conglomeration of rocks fell down from the ceiling, separating her from the others.

"Kal!" It was Max – her voice drowned out by the sound of the crashing rocks.

She was trapped. The rest of the vampires – both Nereti's and her own friends – were on the other side of the barrier. She was alone with Nereti.

Or was she?

A dark figure she had not noticed earlier was standing silently in the shadows. Slowly, calmly, he stepped into the light of the candelabra.

Her heart skipped a beat.

It was Octavius. He was as desperately, devastatingly handsome as ever, his broad shoulders powerful, his taut muscles rippling, the sweat glinting from his tanned, toned chest. He was shirtless, his long dark hair in sensuous tresses, his mouth as wickedly seductive as ever, the thick lips curved in an intoxicating pout. Against herself, Kalina felt the sudden compulsion to run to him, to embrace him, to bury herself in his arms. Surely the sight of her must bring back old feelings – old goodness?

But there was no love for her in his eyes. Nor was there even the slightest bit of desire – or recognition. His eyes were glassy and blank: a cold, cruel stare.

Nereti laughed, a laugh that was almost a cackle. "My general has no interest in you, Imposter," she said. "Octavius doesn't feel the same way about you anymore. He is now my loyal general. He listens to, answers, serves, services, pleasures...only me."

Kalina hadn't expected it to hurt this much. She'd suffered Octavius' betrayal nightly in her dreams, but the sight of him here, in the flesh, was overwhelming.

She needed him like she needed oxygen. But she couldn't touch him. She couldn't kiss him. She couldn't make him hers.

And anger flooded through her once again.

Nereti had taken everything – but this, *this*, she would not let her take.

Blood Curse (Pulse #8)

She would fight.
She would kill.
She would win.

Chapter 12

Kalina felt the rush of blood through her veins like a tidal wave. It wasn't the ordinary beating of her heart – the solemn and straightforward rhythm, like that of a drum beat by marchers off to war. This was something utterly different – utterly profound. Her heart was not merely thumping, not merely pounding, no. In fact, she couldn't even hear the beat at all, so quick was it to pump blood through her veins. It was like a tsunami of blood, a storm of energy coursing through her so quickly that the beating of the heart almost seemed irrelevant – she was beating everywhere; everywhere, she was pulsing with new strength. Everywhere, she was alive.

Seeing Octavius awakened something new in her, something violent. She was overcome with emotion, physical, palpable. She gazed upon his form – shirtless, he glistened, his muscles rippling in the vague and shadowy light of the catacombs. She could make out every single one of his muscles, each abdominal bulge perfectly formed. Against herself, she found herself licking her lips, shocked by her own desire. Her Life's Blood was acting up now – that much she knew. It was making her more susceptible than ever to that profound erotic need that took hold of her body, of her mind, of her senses. Even watching him there with Nereti, there loving the woman she despised, she could not bring herself to feel angry with him. Instead, she felt an imperious and triumphant jealousy – she *would* bring Octavius back to life, back to sense, back to her. Not even Nereti, wicked and cruel, would be able to stop the force of her love.

Her mind was racing. Her body was shuddering. Even now, all she wanted was for Octavius to rush to her, to take her into his powerful and sinewy arms, to kiss her so violently that she screamed. She wanted to feel him inside her, moving between her thighs, splitting her in two with the irascible force of his need. Even now, all she could think about was having him. She had had him before, of course – possessing Nereti's body, she had felt every move of his flesh against her flesh, every little moment of fire and electricity that passed between them. But now, as she caught Octavius out of the corner of her eye, she knew that all that she had experienced in her mind's eye was nothing, absolutely nothing, in comparison with the real thing. She didn't simply want to make love to Octavius telepathically. She wanted to make love to him in the flesh, to give him everything. At that moment she felt, despite herself, that she would sacrifice all the power of her Life's Blood if it meant holding him in her arms again.

But there was only one way to do that. There was only one way to bring Octavius back from the brink, to shock him back into consciousness. She would have to defeat Nereti. She would have to destroy her power, once and for all.

She could not even feel fear. Her adrenaline coursing through her had seen to that. She could not worry about her own life, her own body, whether or not Nereti would break her, drain her, destroy her as she had done to so many other Carriers throughout the years. She had to believe – she had to let her Life's Blood *make* her believe – that she was a power as palpable, as invulnerable, as her nemesis. She had to let herself believe that she, too, might be Queen.

"You fool," Nereti's voice was sweet and sticky, like honey spilled upon a marble floor. "You think he wants you, now? He has seen the error of his ways. He knows what a real woman can offer him – a real woman, like me. Not an indecisive little virgin accustomed to *fooling around.* He knows the pleasures of the flesh, dead or undead. He is done with you."

Kalina caught sight of Octavius' face, of his eyes. If only she could see *something*, she thought desperately, some glint in his eyes, some change in his expression, that might reveal that he still felt something for her, that there was a power in him that could rebel against the spell Nereti had put him under – then she would know that he loved her still.

But he betrayed nothing. His eyes were glassy and vacant. There was no hatred, no anger, no fear, no nothing. There was only a dull and neutral look – the look of a living doll.

"If you're so sure he wants you," Kalina's voice dripped with sarcasm. "Then why don't you unglamour him? If you're as special as you say, he shouldn't need to be transformed into a zombie to want you."

Nereti's mouth thinned into a tight, hard smile. "Insolent girl," she muttered. "Do not speak of what does not concern you."

"Why?" Kalina felt her face grow hot with anger. "Are you scared? Are you afraid that if you let Octavius off his leash, you'll find that he doesn't want you anymore? Is that the only way you know how to keep a man – with magic?"

Nereti's laugh was terrible as it echoed around the caves. "Says the girl whose power lies in the magic of your blood!" She snorted. "You think you're special, after all? That all the vampires between Mongolia and Mont Blanc love you because of *you*?

143

No, my sweet. You're just a source of blood to them. Of sweet, tasty, Carrier-borne Life's Blood. That's all you ever were to Octavius. To Jaegar. To all those foolish brothers who lost their heads over you as a dog might for meat from a bloody bone."

Her insult had landed. Kalina felt the blow deep within her heart. Nereti was lying – she knew she was lying! – she knew Octavius had loved her, that Jaegar loved her...

But Nereti looked so confident, so sure, as she watched Kalina react to the sting.

"But no more talking," she murmured. "You don't want to waste the last moments of your life in idle conversation, do you?"

"Not a chance," said Kalina through gritted teeth.

At once they were at war. At once, Nereti was gliding through the air, her lithe limbs slicing through the empty space between them, her rippling muscles taut.

As much as she despised Nereti, Kalina felt a sense of awe. She was in the presence of a great warrior – of an ancient power – she could feel Nereti's power all around her. How could any woman, how could any *vampire,* be so graceful, so strong?

Help me. Kalina closed her eyes, trying to tap into the power of the Life's Blood within. *Carriers past, present, and future – hear my plea. Let me tap into your strength. Let me be strong enough to bear this.*

Suddenly, she felt as if her whole body were shaking. No longer did she move by her own will, by her own choice. Something else was controlling her body – a force as powerful as that she sensed lurked within Nereti's muscular frame. It was her Life's Blood, boiling, coursing, nearly bursting her veins, carrying within the red blood cells memories of Carriers old and new, of that ancient race of women who had given their lives to fighting against evil.

She heard a murmuring all around her – echoes of whispers. Names of women who had fought, and suffered, and died. Names of women who had loved. Names of all those Carriers who had given everything to get a plague like Nereti off the face of the earth forever.

Kalina began to fight.

She matched Nereti blow for blow, feint for feint, dodge for dodge. She was agile as she sidestepped every attack; she was powerful as she struck Nereti clear across the face, causing the latter to stumble back. She had never felt more natural, more in tune, more in the flow, than she felt in this single moment. She didn't even have to think. Her body knew what to do.

"What...power....is....this?" Nereti was spluttering, her face a mask of shock.

Kalina knew what she was thinking – she could sense it, too; all her powers of telepathy had been heightened, endowing her with a new and strange consciousness.

Who is this girl? Why can she fight like this – when no mortal, Carrier or otherwise, can fight like this? What is her secret? Why is she so strong?

It was something Nereti had never before experienced. Fear. She was fighting harder, fighting longer – fighting, for the first time in her centuries of

146

existence, for her life.

"You never had to try before, did you?" Kalina heard herself speaking. "You're used to slaughtering the innocent, bullying those weaker than you?" She spat on the ground. "Well, your time's up. This time, you'd better give it everything you got. Because this time, you know you're not going to win."

"Lies!" growled Nereti.

"Never lost a battle, have you, Nereti?" Kalina felt herself growing in confidence. "Until now?"

They went on fighting, attacking each other with a hungry violence. Skin met skin, bone met bone; the crunch of bodies slamming against bodies echoed over and over again throughout the chamber.

It went on for hours – but Kalina felt no pain. Her body was bruised, perhaps some bones had been broken, but she could hardly feel them. She was in a new place, a new plane of consciousness. Her Blood had made her strong; nothing else mattered. She was protected by the Blood.

At last, Kalina felt a powerful blow aimed directly at her chest – Nereti had kicked Kalina squarely at the heart, sending her flying backwards with a blow so strong that Kalina shattered the rocks that barred the entry to the cave.

She was on the floor, at the feet of Jaegar, Max, and the others.

"Kal!" Justin cried in relief.

"No time!" shouted Max. "Our turn."

They ran through the new opening to the cave towards Nereti, brandishing their stakes, ready to fight, ready to destroy.

Kalina was reeling. For a moment she felt dizzy, vertiginous, as the force of the blow realigned her consciousness.

Stay strong, Kalina. Stay alive.

But another pair of hands was upon her now, pulling her out of the rubble, helping her to her feet, hands at once soft and so, so strong. Hands that were holding her tightly, caressing her, making her skin cry out in ecstasy.

She turned to see the source of such pleasure.

Her mouth fell open in surprise. His eyes, blazing and dark, were fixed upon her with a look of utter love – one that made her weak at the knees, even now.

Even now, she loved him.

"Octavius?"

Chapter 13

Pain, everywhere. Pain, searing through her skin, her muscles, her spine. Pain, tearing at her limbs, racking her bones apart, sawing through her brain so decisively that for a moment Kalina could not breathe, could not see, could not even think. She had never felt such agony before. The vertebrae in her back were crying out – had she broken her back, she wondered in horror? She couldn't move; she was completely paralyzed, every limb refusing her command.

But none of that mattered now.

Everything had stopped.

Octavius was looking into her eyes, and everything had stopped. Nothing else could matter now. The battle was raging on outside her field of vision; Max and Justin, Samson and Jaegar were fending Nereti off in the distance, but she could hardly even think of that. All she could think about was the fact that at last, at last, Octavius was with her. His blazing, dark eyes were gazing down upon her, their expression unmistakable and full of love. His hair, long and matted, shining like a colt's flank, was falling down over her face, lightly caressing her skin as the hairs moved in the dank breeze of the caves. His hands were tight and firm upon her skin, eliciting the familiar sigh, the familiar moan of pleasure that she could not resist surrendering to him every time he drew near. Oh, how she wanted him!

She could forgive him everything, she thought. She could forgive him his time with Nereti, the passion the two of them had shared, his betrayal: she would forgive him everything, if he would only hold her tighter. If he would only kiss her the way he used to – the spicy darkness of his mouth upon her own.

"Octavius?" she heard herself whisper. "Octavius, my love – what are you doing?"

She hoped that her voice might bring him back to himself. If he heard her, she thought desperately, if he recognized that voice, then maybe he could break the spell, maybe he could recognize the love she still felt for him, and which he had once felt so strongly for her.

One by one, she felt her vertebrae heal – the power of Life's Blood coursing through her to repair every bone, sew up every wound, a sudden sting that made her wince with pain as tears came to her eyes. Her body was preparing itself for another fight.

But as she raised herself up on her elbows, gazing into Octavius' mesmerizing face, she noted with a pang the familiar glassy look in his eyes – the dull, dazed look of enchantment.

No! She wouldn't let him give in – she wouldn't let him succumb to Nereti's wiles. Deep down, she knew, Octavius was still the same man; he was still the vampire who loved her. He had caught her, hadn't he? He had held her, when she had needed him?

She placed one hand on either side of his face; she leaned her forehead against his, making sure his dark, unfathomable eyes caught every angle of her own. She took him in, hoping that he could read within the intensity of her stare all her love, all her desire, all her need.

His pupils began to dilate – as though, Kalina thought with some strange hope – a switch had gone off in him; as if in an instant he had gone from dullness to conscious thought.

"I..." his voice was vague, disembodied. "...I don't know why I'm holding you like this."

She watched his eyes dart back and forth; she watched the stoic look upon his face change into something like pain. She felt his confusion, the conflicting forces that seemed poised to rend him in two. She wanted to comfort him, to take away all his pain, all the conflict that dogged him now.

"Octavius," she whispered, feeling the welling tears overflow the measure of her eyes, snaking their way down the sides of her cheeks. "Oh, Octavius!" She leaned in to kiss him all over: his forehead, his cheeks, his hands, wanting so badly to let her lips tend towards his lips. "My love, I never thought I'd see you again."

The emotion was too great for her to bear. She could not control it. At once she was weeping, sobbing, crying out as if she would never stop. Nothing else mattered now – nothing but the feeling of his flesh on hers; nothing but the man she loved, and thought she had lost, so close, so far, but *with her*, at last. That was all that mattered, she thought desperately. He was with her.

Then she began to feel something strange. Beneath her palms, his cheeks felt – warmer? No, that was impossible – vampires were cold, always, cold like the frozen caves of the North. But what she felt was unmistakable. It was warm skin, warm, solid flesh – the flesh of mortal love, mortal heat, mortal desire.

"I..." Octavius' words were still so confused. "I don't understand. My blood – it's moving – it's pulsing – it recognizes yours."

"What?"

"It's stronger – it's the strongest blood of all." He was looking at her with a fixed and intense expression. "It's so much stronger than *hers*."

Kailin Gow

Then it hit Kalina. Then she understood. Understood why she had been able to predict Nereti's movements, to match her blow for violent blow as they fought. Nereti had been filled with Kalina's blood – she had drained her almost to death back at the ruins in the desert. It might have made her stronger – but it also had opened in her a new weakness. Kalina's Life Blood had affected Nereti, to be sure, but it hadn't simply given her new power. It had also given her a bond with Nereti, a bond unlike any other. Kalina was different from the other Carriers, after all. She'd had Nereti's blood in her from birth. And now Nereti had her blood, too. A double-bond of blood, stronger than any other that had ever existed. It was as though they were twins, dark mirrors of one another, two sides of the same coin.

One good. One evil.

Or so she hoped.

"Octavius..." Her voice was growing desperate now. "Octavius, my darling, my love, do you remember me?"

155

Blood Curse (Pulse #8)

For a long time he looked at her, his gaze ever more intense, staring at every single one of her features, staring into her eyes, as if trying to recover the vanished images of a dream. He began to shake his head – a long, slow rotation – but stopped, his mouth slightly parted, his eyes still so direct upon her. "Yes," he whispered at last. "Yes, I do."

She could not stop herself. Before she had even taken in his words, she had flung herself upon him. She was kissing him, kissing him so hard and so violently, kissing him as she had never kissed him – or anybody else – before.

At first he was reluctant. He did not push her away, but he did not return her kiss either. He remained stoic and still, considering.

But her warmth kindled his. At once he grabbed her, his fingers twisting in the obsidian darkness of her hair, pulling her towards him, kissing and kissing her with a hungry mouth, his desire palpable in every motion, every electric collision of their flesh.

"Remember this?" she breathed, barely able to

break away from him long enough to answer the question.

He pulled her in for another kiss, even more ravenous than before, his lips violent and voracious upon her own. "How could I forget?" he whispered. "My love, my heart."

"Did you forget me?" she couldn't help asking. "All that time you were with...*her*, with Nereti. Did you forget I existed?"

His eyes were full of pain. "It was the only thing that kept me sane," he growled. "Nereti had me under her control – she controlled my mind, my body, my limbs, everything about me. It was like I was drugged, in a haze or a fog, not the master of my own body or even my own thoughts. But deep down, I knew. Deep down, I knew that she could never control my heart. Even when I couldn't remember your face, your voice, your name, my heart remembered the memory of you – remembered that there was someone I loved, outside of this wretched world of me and her – remembered that there was something worth maintaining my sanity before."

"But you and she..."

"I never spoke of you to her. I never wanted her to suspect that I had some element of consciousness outside her control. I was afraid that if she knew another had my heart, she would try another spell, one that would make me forget you entirely. So I went along with her deception – to keep you safe, to keep all of you safe. Sadly, so many noble vampires of the Consortium were sacrificed in her wicked wake. For that, I will forever bear the guilt. I will bear the burden of that regret, along with the ashen remains of the sacrificed, for all eternity. I will bear the searing memories of the time I spent in Nereti's bed – the wild pleasure and the deadly shame. Her pull was overwhelming – this I will not deny. But it was wicked, through and through – and every moment I spent with her I was aware I was in the presence of the greatest evil, of the Mother of Vampires."

"The Mother of Vampires?" Kalina's mouth fell open. "What does that mean?"

"She is the oldest vampire ever born. Born,

not made. Not like the rest of us. That is why Carrier blood is so strong – it contains the blood of this ancient type."

"How did you learn this? I've never heard of a vampire being born."

"Nor had I. But when I was with her – in bed – in moments of her greatest pleasure, she showed me telepathic glimpses of the world she had come from, the world of her origin, an ancient world utterly unlike our own, where all the myths we can imagine are but the most prosaic realities, and their myths so much greater still than any which we can think of. When she – when she climaxed, she revealed it to me."

Kalina grimaced. She didn't like thinking about Octavius and Nereti, giving one another pleasure in that way.

"What is this place?"

"Not of this earth, Kal. It is a realm of magic, of fantasy, of beings with teeth and blood-lust, where vampires are more of an abomination than they have ever been in this realm...."

He was cut off by a shout from the caves. Nereti had pinned Justin and Jaegar to the wall of the cave. They were crying out, wriggling against her superior strength, as she readied her hand to plunge into the chest of one or the other, to pull out their heart.

"No!" Kalina cried in horror.

But Octavius was faster.

In a lightning-flash he had knocked the others aside, placed himself squarely in Nereti's path.

It was only when her hand was deep inside his chest that Nereti realized what she had done.

"Octavius?" Now it was her voice that was full of confusion.

Nereti stopped, and stared, her hands overflowing with blood.

"No!" Kalina cried again. The horror, the anger was too great. She was flying through the air, ready to attack, ready to defend.

Her mind had gone blank.

She would save Octavius.

That was all she knew.

Chapter 14

For a moment, everything was still – horribly, preternaturally still. All Kalina could hear was the sound of the cave – the dripping of water deep within the belly of the cavern, the hollow wind rustling lamely through the labyrinthine corridors, the lonely scratches of mice and other beasts in the furthest reaches of the cavern's depths. For a moment, Kalina's mind went blank.

She was focusing on the littlest things, on the strangest things. She was focusing on Octavius' face, and the look of pain in his deep and blazing eyes, on precisely how his nose curled so slightly at the base. She was focusing on Nereti's porcelain countenance, on the way Nereti's left eyebrow was arched upwards in shock as she took in the full force of what she had done: as she realized that her hand was wrist-deep in Octavius' chest, gorging with blood that overflowed up her forearm, staining it dark, wine-dark.

"No..." Kalina whispered in horror, feeling the pounding in her own chest grow louder, ever louder, with despair. Octavius had saved Justin and Jaegar's life – but at what cost? Was this how it was going to end – *could* this be how it ended – Octavius murdered by the woman who had already taken so much from him, who had already made him her slave?

Nereti's expression was gradually changing, the features contorting in slow motion. She had previously sported a look of utter fury; now that fury was muted. Instead her face bore the signs of shock, of horror, even of fear. Quickly, with the nimble lightness that befit her status as Mother of Vampires, she withdrew her bloodied hand from Octavius' broad chest, from which now gushed forth new torrents.

For a moment, she stood in shock – utter shock. Kalina looked at her in wonder. She had never seen Nereti so shaken, so overcome by anything at all.

But then Nereti regained control of her body.

She immediately took both of her palms and placed them against Octavius' chest, against the sweat and the skin. No sooner had she done so than a glowing golden light appeared, radiating outward from her fingertips. The light shone upon the wound.

Slowly, surely, the skin began to close together; the wound began to heal. Kalina could see Octavius' face – how the pain was slowly leaving him, replaced instead with slightly dazed self-possession. Octavius was being restored to life.

It hit Kalina like a thunderstorm. All at once she began to hear Nereti's thoughts, loud as cannons, landing surefire into her brain.

What am I doing? This is not like you, Nereti. This is not behavior befitting the Mother of Vampires. You are above all things, higher in your solitude than all desires. You are the mistress of yourself, and no man has ever defeated you on the battlefield. No man has ever defeated you. You are strong; you are ancient; you possess the old and atavistic forces of the old world. You have never once faltered. Never once have you shown mercy.

Blood Curse (Pulse #8)

Until now.

Kalina heard the echo; it reverberated in her brain.

Until now. Until now. Until now.

You do not love him. He is your minion, nothing more. He is a source of pleasure, a mere toy. If he dies you will have another. There is nothing special about him, nothing singular, nothing to be preserved. What could possibly make you think that you have anything for him except the knowledge that you are Queen and he is merely Subject. You owe him nothing.

You do not love him.

But why have you saved him, then?

He was defiant – he stayed your hand – is this alone not reason enough to rip out his heart and stamp it beneath your feet, beneath your heel that has stamped out so many thousands and turned their broken bodies into ash and dirt? He deserves to die, Nereti.

But you wished to save him.

You saw the pain in his eyes, and you wished to take it away.

164

You saw the blood in his chest, and you wished to close the wound.

You saw him weakened, and this is what you do?

You – who never once have felt fear – you feared losing this man, this vampire, this rogue? It cannot be.

Nereti's face was a mask. Her expression betrayed nothing. Her lips, ruby-dark, were pursed; her eyes were staring straight ahead in imperious triumph. But Kalina knew her secret, now.

Nereti had feelings for Octavius. She didn't know where they came from, what they were, what they even meant, but she knew – true as anything – that they were there. Not that she could blame Nereti – she knew all too well the intoxicating effect of Octavius on those who came into contact with him. But to spur an evil being like Nereti into doing an act of good?

You have never in your life healed. You have only destroyed. This golden light – it is strange to you – you do not know it. You heard tell of it, when you

165

lived in that other world, that other creatures of your kith and kin could undo the damage that you'd done, could create when you could only destroy.

Do you miss it, Nereti? Do you miss that other world, that world which you once knew and which you once called home? Do you wish you were there again, there in a place that you truly belonged to, that you loved so much that you never needed conquer it, for it was yours already, a part of your soul? There was a time when you were not wicked. There was a time when you were not cruel. There was a time when you were in a place where you belonged, and that place was home.

But where is all that now? Is not that self gone, vanished, broken beyond repair? You are no longer that young girl, that young immortal being, alive with the promise of her immortality, among the gardens of the Old Place, smelling the flowers that were scattered around you as you walked, smelling the clean air high where the trees did not even grow, watching the twin suns dapple the light in the sky all around you.

It is gone.

You are wicked, now; that is all you are.
All of this is gone.

Kalina felt her muscles tense up. Now was the time, she knew; now was the moment to strike. Nereti was distracted – perhaps for the first and only time in her long, long life.

She let the blow fall. She let the Life's Blood course through her, giving her new strength. Her kick sent Nereti flying across the cavern, landing straight into a pile of rocks, her body a projectile breaking them apart.

Nereti screamed as the rocks fell down around her.

Immediately Kalina was at Octavius' side. It was her turn to tend him, now. She felt her desire meld with true compassion, true love for this man who had saved the lives of those she cared about, who had even risked his own. She pressed her hand against her forehead; she kissed his cheeks, his neck, his shoulders. She kissed all of him, hoping that he would feel her love.

"Are you all right?" she breathed.

Blood Curse (Pulse #8)

He looked up at her, adoration in his eyes. "Better," he said, his voice hoarse with the memory of pain. "Much better now that you are here, my darling."

How can this be? Nereti's voice was still so strong in Kalina's head. *The bitch is still alive. How is it that I cannot defeat her? How is it that she returns from the very brink of destruction, always to torment me again? It is as if there is some magic in her that prevents my killing her – it is as if the ancient forces themselves have determined that I shall not be victorious. Look at her, how she stands, with my General under her hands. Look how he looks up at her, like a sick little puppy dog, how he gives her all his adoration, all his need. How is it that he loves her so? How is it that he has chosen her over me? What is so special about this girl, this mere mortal, this slip of a thing, that makes her worth choosing over me, me the Mother of Vampires?*

Her jealousy lit a fire in Kalina's heart. She was pleased, deep down, to know that Nereti considered her such a threat. But she felt, too, a

168

pang of compassion for the goddess – a goddess who had at once shown her human side.

Kalina tensed, bracing herself for the next attack. Nereti would strike back – of this she had no doubt.

But to her surprise, Nereti was rising high, faster than lightning, flying away from the cave.

Was she running away in retreat? Was she afraid?

Then Kalina heard an echo of Nereti's thoughts. *If I cannot kill her, perhaps these cave walls will. Even if it is not given to me to have victory, nature will take its course.*

What did that mean? Kalina looked around, wildly.

Then she noticed it. The cracks in the cave walls. The trembling fractures. The walls were about to crumble – to bury them all inside!

"No!" she cried out. "We have to get..."

But Nereti's thoughts were getting louder again, getting ncarer.

You cannot leave him. You cannot leave this

General, although you do not know why. You know only that he cannot die like the others, you must save him...

Nereti was coming back.

"Run!" Kalina cried.

But Nereti was already upon them, her wrist tight around Octavius' wrist.

"Back off!" Kalina heard herself shouting. "Can't you understand, woman? Octavius isn't under your control any longer? He doesn't want you!"

"Like it or not," Nereti spat back, "he will be, and soon you all will be under my control, too. Look around you, fool, the walls are crumbling down. Soon you will all be trapped here for ages, and nobody will know – no one except."

She grabbed Octavius, poised to fly out with him – but Octavius had grabbed Kalina's wrist, too.

By the time the rocks came tumbling down, all three of them had been pulled from the rubble.

"Max!" Kalina cried out. "Justin!"

But it was too late. They had vanished beneath the rubble. Whether they were alive or dead

Kalina could not know. All that she knew was that she was flying through the air with Octavius and Nereti, higher and higher; that she was leaving the rest of them behind.

Chapter 15

Kalina's heart began to beat faster and faster as terror coursed through her veins. What had happened? The shock of the incident had hit her all at once. She had been fighting Nereti – she had been winning – she had at last made a show of superior strength. And then in an instant Nereti had outsmarted her. Nereti had lured her away – she had been prepared to go in for the final blow, to kill Nereti at last – but at what cost? Behind her, beneath her, all around her – the boulders had collapsed. The cave had crumbled. All those she had loved were buried within the cavernous expanses of the labyrinth. She could not hear their voices – either with her ears or with her mind. She could not think. Her mind had gone blank, as blank as the desert.

Her body kept on flying, chasing after Nereti, going faster and faster, but her mind wasn't there at all. She was vague, detached; her anger was directionless; her hatred of Nereti had rendered her virtually unaware of all that was happening around her.

And then she heard it. The cry. The cry of the man she loved, echoing through her eardrums.

Kalina.

Jaegar's voice. Jaegar's low, deep voice – the sound of which made her melt, made her knees weak and her heart beat too fast for her to stand. Jaegar was alive – Jaegar was fine.

At once she forgot her mission. At once she forgot her promise to destroy Nereti, whatever the cost. She had to go back – to help Jaegar, to save him, to save the others.

No.

Jaegar's voice was determined, full of pain. She could hear the tears in his voice.

What do you mean, no? I've got to come back. I've got to save you.

No. The voice again, as steely as a sword. *You are the Chosen Girl. You must fulfill your mission.*

173

That is more important than any of us. You must leave us – now. You must destroy Nereti.

I have to save you!

You have to save the world.

Kalina felt herself pulled in two different directions – a pull so strong it almost caused her physical pain. The wrenching in her heart was too great for her to bear. Part of her wanted to keep chasing after Nereti, to destroy her now while she still had the chance, to kill her now that she had the advantage. Who could say when she'd ever get the upper hand again? And Jaegar was right – how many people, innocent people, would be killed if she didn't stop Nereti in time. The fate of the whole world hung in the balance – she knew that. *Of course* she knew that.

And yet...

How could she leave Jaegar behind? How could she leave any of those she loved – Max, Justin, her mother and her brother – how could she say goodbye to them like this, leaving them to their fate?

You have to save the world.

Jaegar's voice was firm, strong. He did not allow for any other option. She had to leave him behind – she had to say goodbye – she had to do what was best...

Then she heard Jaegar's voice drifting – he wasn't speaking to her, now, but to someone else. *Max, Max, hold on, please hold on. Samson – Samson, where are you? We need your help. We need to lift this boulder...*

Kalina's heart stopped within her chest. Max – hurt? Max – trapped beneath a boulder? The image was so strong within her mind that she felt as if she had received it telepathically: an image of Max, of her mother, trapped, pinned to the floor, blood trickling from the corners of her mouth.

Max? What's wrong with Max?

Kalina heard the silence that was worse than any word could have been. She waited, her heart refusing to so much as beat, for a reply.

Kalina – you need to go! You need to chase after Nereti!

Not until you tell me what happened.

Blood Curse (Pulse #8)

She's hurt. It's fine – she'll be okay.

She won't, will she?

Another silence – another silence she could hardly stand.

I don't know. It's pretty bad. She was crushed by a boulder.

She was a Carrier. She was a human. She was not an immortal. It hit Kalina, all at once. *Max could die.*

Any other human would have died immediately. But Max is strong. She's got Life's Blood in her. But...I don't know if it's going to be enough. She still has a pulse --- but I don't know how long it's going to last. Her bones are broken; her vital organs have been crushed.

Everything went white. Kalina couldn't see, couldn't think, couldn't feel. All she could experience was an all-consuming pain. She couldn't think of Max dying – how could she possibly think of that? Max was so strong – she was invincible, wasn't she? So brave, so powerful. And she was *her mother.*

Kalina remembered how it had been to lose

176

her adopted mother – the woman she had known as "Mom" her whole life. She remembered how much she had loved her, how hard it had been. And then she'd had another mother enter her life – a mother she'd never known – a mother she'd never fully understood. But a mother all the same. She'd lost her mother, her father, Justin, too, in a way – to the world of the vampires. She couldn't lose another family member.

She knew the decision had already been made.

Octavius – I can't go on. I have to go back.

She dropped his hand before waiting for his reply. He might try to stop her, she thought. He might try to make her do the same thing Jaegar wanted her to do – to leave them all behind.

She wouldn't. She couldn't. There were some things even heroes shouldn't have to do.

She was flying faster than she had ever flown before. She was bullet-fast through the air, whipping through it, letting the sands scratch at her face as she plummeted back towards the rubble.

Blood Curse (Pulse #8)

Out of the corner of her eye she spotted Jaegar and Justin, their faces wrenched with pain, as they were pushing against a boulder the size of a small hill. Beneath the stone was a body – so small, Kalina thought; she'd never seen Max look so small. Her eyes were closed; her skin was waxy, sickly, white. Kalina didn't look at her – she *couldn't* look at her. One look at Max, lying there like that, and she'd burst into tears.

She leaned her hands against the boulder and began to push. It almost gave way, creaking slightly, but even with the three of them there they weren't strong enough.

"Where's Justin?" Jaegar asked impatiently.

"I don't know," replied Justin. "We've already searched everywhere. I've tried telepathy – I've tried shouting – I've tried everything! I can't get hold of him. Maybe he's been knocked unconscious...or worse...."

"Then we have to try harder." Kalina gritted her teeth. "We can't let Max stay here. We have to get her out."

Jaegar's eyes were full of pain. "I'm so sorry, Kal," he whispered. "I don't want to be the one to tell you this..."

"Tell me what?"

"Even vampire strength – it's nothing against nature. Nature is more powerful than any of us – you know that."

"What does that mean?"

"This boulder's the size of a mountain, Kal. Pure stone. Even vampire strength won't cut it."

"Kal..." The voice was wheezy, whispered. Max croaked out a final sigh.

"Max?" Kalina rushed to her side. "Max – stay awake, talk to me!"

But it was too late. Max had closed her eyes, passing out from the pain.

"Well, we can't leave her here!" Tears were streaming down Kalina's face.

Jaegar's voice was full of pain. "I'm so sorry, Kal. Max means so much to all of us – you know that – she's family to all of us, now."

"And you'll just give up on her?" Kalina's pain

179

had turned to anger. "After all she's done for you – you'll just give up?"

"I don't want to..."

"And here I thought..."

Kalina wasn't even sure what she had wanted to say. In an instant, Jaegar's lips were upon hers, kissing hungrily, sublimating his pain into desire, a kiss that felt like he was trying to remember it, to savor it, to drown in her lips.

Then he pulled away violently, ramming into the boulder with all his strength.

It lifted with a thud.

"Quickly!" Jaegar cried out. "Justin, Kal! Lift it so we can get Max."

It lifted enough for Kalina to stick her hand underneath before it collapsed again, with Kalina barely removing her hand just in time.

"We've got to pray..." whispered Justin. His face had gone the color of chalk.

Kalina had never thought to pray before. Her experiences with vampires had pushed all other thoughts of the world beyond this one out of her mind. But now, as desperation flooded through her, she had no other choice. With her eyes closed and her hands together, she began to mutter, whispering her pleas.

Jaegar gritted his teeth and with lightning speed ran back towards the entrance of the cave and back to the rock, ramming it as hard as he could so that it made an explosive sound and caused the rock to slightly lift up again.

"Holy son of a...." Justin's voice rose in surprise.

The boulder began to lift higher.

To Kalina's surprise, Samson was standing before them, lifting the boulder, his strength worthy of that of his namesake.

"Help me push!" he cried in a hoarse voice. "One, two, three."

The boulder lifted just enough for Kalina to pull Max out from underneath.

She looked different – so different. She had aged in an instant. Her long raven hair was brittle and gray; wrinkles lined her once-porcelain cheeks.

"Mom!" Kalina enveloped Max with her arms. "Mom, are you okay? We need to get her to the hospital! We need to get her better! Hurry!" She bared her wrist, preparing to bite into it, to give Max the Life's Blood she needed.

"Stop!" Justin put a warning hand on Kalina's shoulder.

"She's still breathing!" Kalina cried, pressing her hands upon her mother's chest. "Mom, no, I need you – I've found you now. I need you to pull through. For me. For Justin. For all of us. Please, please..."

"Kalina, you need to stop..." Justin's voice was low and full of agony. "She's gone. It's over."

"She's not! She's breathing! I can tell – she's fine! She's going to be all right. Mom, mom, can you hear me?"

But no answer came.

Chapter 16

Pain shot through her like a bullet, drowning out all conscious thought. How could this be? She had already lost one mother, borne the pain and heartbreak of losing her and her father in one fell swoop. She had already mourned. And now here she was, being asked to mourn anew, to lose the mother – the second mother – she had only just gained. No, it couldn't be real, Kalina thought desperately. It mustn't be real. This woman, this mother – she would save her, couldn't she save her? She had saved so many others, after all – she had to be able to save the woman she cared for more than any other woman in the world.

Justin was kneeling at Max's side, a mournful expression on his face. His fingers were pressed against her pulse. "She's alive..." he whispered hoarsely, "but only just. She's in a really bad way, Kalina. I don't know that there's much hope, that there's any hope at all..."

No, it couldn't be! Max was so full of life, so full of strength. Max couldn't be dying – not like this.

There was one thing she could do, she thought wildly. There was one – only one – way out of this. She bared her own wrist, her teeth shining in the moonlight as she prepared to open up her own veins, to feed her mother the Life's Blood that she knew could save her, could it only save her.....

"No!" Justin's hand was firm and tight upon her wrist. "Kal, you can't."

"But it's the only way," Kalina heard herself cry. "It's the only way to save her."

"You don't know the consequences of your actions, Kalina," Justin said darkly. "I know you want to save her. I do too....but we can't..."

"Why not? She's a Carrier, isn't she? With strong Life's Blood in her veins? I could have saved her, I know it. I could give her my blood, help her get her strength back."

"She may have been a Carrier," Justin's voice was gentle but authoritative. "But she was also a

184

human being. A human being with a human heart, human bones, human skin. Injuries that would have been too great, too painful, for any human to bear."

"But my blood would have saved her!"

"It would have kept her alive, yes," Justin looked down, pain welling up in his eyes. "But is that really healing? If her bones were crushed, her internal organs destroyed – she would be alive, but would she ever be out of pain? Or would she be a vegetable, condemned to suffer for all eternity!"

"It isn't like that!" Kalina cried. "I don't care – she'd be alive!"

"Remember what Stuart said about vampires when they are immortal, and met with nature? When we were in the plane, when it was going down – they were so afraid to survive, because the pain of eternal life when your body is that badly damaged is the worst fate of all. Pain and aching, all your days – excruciating pain so bad you couldn't even think or act – is that what you want for her, Kal?"

Even now, Kalina thought, Justin was the consummate doctor – delivering difficult news with such a calm and gentle manner that she couldn't even feel angry with him. He must have delivered news like this to his patients before. But that was very different from delivering it to her.

"It can't be..." But she knew this was no longer true.

"I'm afraid it is," Justin said.

"After all this..."

Normally Kalina could handle her emotions, but not today. Her Life's Blood was boiling, burning, in a way that it had never burned even for Jaegar or Octavius. This bond was stronger than any bond of desire. It was the bond of mother and daughter, of blood shared, blood twinned. The bond that every creature had with the mother that bore it. She felt as if she were experiencing Max's pain, Max's agony, as if the boulder were crushing her own organs.

The pain was so powerful that she collapsed.

Around her, she could feel Jaegar's arms, holding her tight, pressing against her, doing all they could to take away her pain.

"No..."

186

Her field of vision had gone blank. Everything was moving, swaying, shuddering, shimmering with the pain.

"Kalina, please, Kal, Kal..." Jaegar was murmuring in her ear. "You have to be strong, Kal. You have to fight that pull. I'm not letting you go, too. I won't let you go. I can't."

*****

Kalina woke up not too long after – at least, if the position of the moon in the sky was anything to go by. But it felt that she had been sleeping for centuries. Her head was heavy; her whole body ached; she felt as if she were supporting hundreds of pounds' worth of weight upon her shoulders.

She awoke to the clanging of swords. She could hear shouts – echoes – murmurs and hisses. What was going on? She craned her neck to see the shadows flitting across the cave walls. Justin and Jaegar had lit a fire, and the firelight made the shadows even darker, even larger.

"Where is our queen?"

The voice was sharp – deep and rough – the voice of a man on the prowl. Sword steel clashed against sword steel in the distance.

"Beats me." Kalina could identify Jaegar's cocky swagger, even without looking at him. "As far as we're all concerned, you can have her anytime you want her. We want nothing to do with her."

"Insolent swine!" The minion's voice careened into a roar. "I'll just have to make you suffer extra hard before you die. I'll break your neck, stomp upon your chest, break all your bones before I stake you...

Jaegar's voice was almost a purr. "Well, you can *try...*"

Kalina sat up straight. She no longer thought of her pain, of her fear, of her worry. She thought only of the need to survive. It made her strong. She reached for her stake, ready to go fight.

Then she saw them.

They were so many of them – so many she could not believe it. A swarm, like maggots or buzzards, descending upon the labyrinth of the caves. At their head was a vampire larger than almost any she had ever seen – taller still even than Octavius – with rippling muscles and hands that looked as if they were formed to tear apart unsuspecting victims. He was fearsome, terrifying. This was no ordinary minion – cannon fodder, sent by Nereti to the slaughter. This was a true rival.

And the vampires he led were no less frightening. With their red eyes and their vicious smiles, they were prepared to wreak as much havoc as possible, and enjoy the pain and suffering they caused.

They stretched across the corridors of the cave and out into the desert sands, black and great dots – like oversized locusts. Nereti's army had come to seek its victory, its queen. They had come for the woman they worshipped.

Kalina had to think fast. They were outnumbered – there was no hope of fighting them off now. Even at full strength it would have been a challenge, and they were hardly at full strength now. Jaegar was injured barely holding it together. She could see the bravado in his eyes, the false courage, but she knew that his injury was too deep for that now. He wouldn't be able to take out more than five or ten vampires at the most. Samson was there, to be sure, and Justin too – an unmistakably human look of terror in his vampire eyes. But Max was lying there with her closed eyes, her wrinkled skin, her long gray hair fanned out around her like a halo. Max was gone – and there was nothing to save them now...

There was only one thing she could do.

She had to use her wits.

She straightened her back, rumpled her hair, assumed the most imperious and cruel expression she could. These minions had never seen Nereti up close – she had to bet on that, that the Queen would never let her lowly attendants near enough to see her face.

She strode out from behind the boulder and assumed an angry glare.

"You swine!" Her voice was not her own. "Must I do everything myself? You come only now, now that

I've fought off hundreds of these rogue vampires. Look at me – I've even ruined my clothing. And you will pay for the amount of time it took you to get here, you worthless fools. Now a mere handful of these rogues are left, without a single knowledge of the diamonds, of what they are and what they can do. We must go after them now. We must get the diamonds – *my* diamonds."

The thrill of adrenaline coursed through her. She couldn't think about anything, now. She had to *be* Nereti, and that was all.

"Diamonds?" The head vampire looked confused.

"Of course diamonds! Minion – whose name I do not care to remember – do you question me?"

The look of terror in her minion's eyes told her that the ruse had been a success. "It does not matter, my Queen," he said. "It is not for me to know. I humbly apologize for our latest, and hope that you spare us. We will march as fast as we can to go after them. Tell us where we need to go and wc shall gu right away."

"To the East!" Kalina exclaimed. Back to Mongolia." She thought quickly. It would take days for them to get there, and only in that cave would they have sufficient rubies to destroy the vampires.

"To the East, then!" The minion bowed and scraped his way out of the cave, his army following behind him.

Kalina looked around in relief. He was gone. The danger was averted. She felt tears of exhaustion stinging at her eyes.

Around her, Samson was smiling, Justin was grinning, and Jaegar – well, Jaegar was looking at her with the greatest joy, the greatest devotion of all. "Sexy *and* smart," he said, his fangs sparkling in the heart of his smile. "That's one of so many reasons that I love you."

Kalina almost smiled, but the sight of Max on the floor, out of the corner of her eye, stopped the smile upon her lips.

And then she noticed it – a trick of the eye, she thought bitterly, designed to prolong her pain. A twitch – no, it wasn't a twitch, just an illusion...

Then Max twitched again.

Chapter 17

Kalina could hardly dare to hope. She had suffered, already, suffered and mourned; her heart had already broken. She had seen Max die; she had felt her – her mother – grow limp and lifeless in her arms. She had watched as those beautiful, piercing blue eyes – the eyes that made her feel so safe, so warm – closed for one final time. She had seen it all and wept.

Surely she must be imagining things! She wanted Max to live so badly – she had hoped so badly for some miracle – that she was making things up, creating illusions, mirages, hallucinations, whatever you called them – all with the same result. She was deluding herself into happiness.

Max was dead. Her mother was dead. Her mother had died for the second time. There was no use in denying it; there was no point in pretending that anything was different. Her mother was dead, and she was an orphan, alone in the world.

But then Max twitched again.

Kalina did not know what to think. She could not bear to think at all. She could only feel – feel her heart patter faster with anticipation, feel her blood boil and rip through her veins, feel her breath grow hot and shallow within her lungs.

Max opened her eyes.

For a moment Kalina stood there, shocked, overwhelmed, overcome, unable to make sense of what she saw. For a moment Kalina remained, convinced that she was lying to herself, that this was only a trick of her mind, a cruel trick her mind was playing on her, to make the pain that much keener, that much sharper, when she realized it again. She could no longer trust her mind. She could no longer trust life to keep her away from pain.

But Max's eyes were open, wide open, and they were staring straight at her.

"Max!" It was Justin's voice that woke Kalina from her stupor. Justin had seen it too – this was no trick – this was no illusion.

Max was alive.

"Mom?" Kalina's own voice sounded parched and strange in her throat. Someone else's voice, it seemed. Not hers. "Mom...are you..."

Are you what? Alive? Okay? She hardly knew what to say. Her lips were dry and cracked with tears.

"K-k-k...." Max's lips were trembling, but the sound made its way out. The first letter of Kalina's name.

"You're alive!" At last Kalina could spring into action, spring into life. "You're alive," she cried again, hardly daring to believe what was happening. She looked up with pleading eyes at Justin. "What do we do? How can we help her?"

Justin's eyes were shining with tears of joy. "I...I don't know.' He stammered. "I mean...I deal with human patients. Normal human patients. This isn't exactly my field..."

"Can we take her to the hospital?"

"I...uh...I mean, I guess that's what you'd do...you know, normally. But Max – I mean, Mom – she's not an ordinary patient, is she? They'd ask a *lot*

196

of questions. And I don't know if things like X-Rays really matter...when it comes to a Carrier. I mean, you're not exactly normal human beings."

Kalina felt the sting. She said nothing, but inwardly she recoiled. It was true, wasn't it – what Justin said? She and Max, whatever they were, weren't human. She knew that, deep down, but somehow she hated to be reminded of it.

Kalina looked up at Jaegar, whose expression was torn. "I could offer her my vampire blood," he ventured softly. "Or you can offer yours."

It wasn't even a question. Before he had finished speaking, Kalina had bitten deeply into her own wrist, letting the pain flood through her as droplets of blood gathered on Max's pale lips. She watched as Max's tongue darted out, as she drank the Life's Blood down.

Then she sat straight up, her eyes wide and bulging. She retched, once, then began to cough violently, vomiting up all the blood in a single, sickening motion.

Kalina's mouth fell open in shock. How could

it be? How and why was Max rejecting Carrier blood?

"Let me try!" Jaegar bit into his own wrist, and fed Max from it. But still Max was rejecting the dark liquid, spitting it up like a recalcitrant baby.

"What's going on?" Jaegar looked almost hurt. "That's a first. Nobody's ever rejected my blood like that before..."

"I don't understand." Kalina's brow furrowed with confusion. "Why is she rejecting our blood?"

Max's coughing grew louder. Her chest racked with the upheaval. At last she was able to make out a few words. "The diamonds..." she whispered, croaking hoarsely, "I need some. My body – it craves..."

Kal looked up at Jaegar in surprise. There were a few diamonds left over, she knew, in the leather pouch he was carrying.

"This?" Jaegar asked her.

"Yes!" Max's voice grew violent. "Give them to me!"

In shock Jaegar handed her the pouch, automatically.

198

Max ripped it open in a single motion.

"Wait!" Jaegar cried. "If it disintegrates vampires – how do we know what it'll do to you?"

"You don't," rasped Max. "But I need it. Now."

She poured the diamonds into her palm. Nothing happened.

Then she swallowed them down whole.

"Mom!" Kalina cried in horror. Surely nobody could survive swallowing diamonds. They were the hardest substance on earth – they would lacerate the organs – they would kill her.

"I can't help it..." Max was shaking. "I must have it. Must...have..."

Jaegar stepped up closer to Max. He showed Kalina her wounds. There, where Max had been crushed, tiny pieces of diamond were embedded into her skin.

"She must have fallen on one of the piles of ash where the vampires were disintegrated," he said softly. He took a twig and brought one of the pieces closer.

"Holy...smokes." He looked up at Kalina in

199

surprise. "It's not a diamond at all...." The piece was glowing a bright white color.

"Whatever it is," Samson said gruffly, "it's working. Look."

Max was no longer desiccated, no longer wrinkly or gray. She was as beautiful, as vibrant as she had ever been.

"What's going on?" Kalina couldn't believe her eyes.

"I don't know..." Max was starting to talk like her old self again. "I think it's one of the elements in the Life's Blood. It must be. There was something like this in the box we found in the doctor's house in China – perhaps it's one of the base ingredients of Life's Blood...."

"I've never seen anything like this before," Justin said.

"It's not of this world," cut in Jaegar authoritatively.

"You mean it's from space?" Kalina turned to him with questioning eyes.

"Possibly," Justin said. "But not likely. I think

– I think it's from a completely different universe altogether. Something...old. Something...magical. Can't you just feel it?" He gave a little laugh. "A couple of years ago, I'd never be talking like this," he said. "I didn't even believe in the supernatural. But now..."

"Everything's different," Kalina echoed him softly.

"It's from the world where the first vampires originated," Jaegar said. "The world where Nereti was born. No wonder she wanted them so badly."

"So that's why she's the only vampire who can handle touching it." Kalina's eyes widened with realization. "Humans can, Carriers can, but not other vampires – except for her. And her kind. Whatever that means. What is her *kind*?" She smiled softly. "All I know about other kinds of vampires I know from the movies. Or from you."

Jaegar laughed. "Humanity needed to explain us. So we're relegated into the media as one kind, one thing. Sparkly vampires excepted, of course. But we're more complicated than that. There are many

201

kinds of vampires....or so I'm starting to think. Because Nereti isn't like us."

"So how do we get to this other world? Where Nereti's from? Is there a portal, a ley line, a gateway...anything?"

"I don't know," said Jaegar. "But we're near some of the oldest places in human civilization. If there were to be a portal, it would be a pretty good guess to suppose it's somewhere around here. Don't you think?"

"Then..." It was all coming together in Kalina's mind. "That's probably what Nereti's trying to find. She's trying to head back there."

"Head back there? Why would she do that?"

"I don't know..." Kalina faltered. "I know her plans were to stay here, to take over humanity, to enslave us all. But she wants something else now, too. She wants to go home. I felt it in her. I saw it in her. When I shared her thoughts. Something different, that made her long for home. I think...I think she was scared."

"Scared?" Jaegar scoffed. "Nereti? I highly

doubt that..."

Samson stepped forward, a serious expression on his face. "What brought *that on?*" He turned to Kalina. "It could be important. What's her weakness?"

"Octavius," Kalina said softly.

Samson and Jaegar looked at one another. For a moment, there was silence. Then both of them burst out into hysterical laughter.

"Good old General!" Samson's laugh was hearty and deep. "I knew he had a plan. I just didn't think he would ever go so far as to..."

"Go so far as to what?" Kalina couldn't understand what was going on. "He had a plan?"

Samson looked over at Jaegar; Jaegar looked down, shuffling his feet. "If you've known the guy for over five centuries," he said, "You'd be pretty sure that he had a plan. He always had a plan. I bet Octavius was born with a plan."

Samson nodded. "Octavius is one of the youngest, the very fiercest, one of the most august and venerated vampire generals for a reason, Kalina.

He is a great leader, a very great leader. He'll do whatever he has to do to fulfill his obligations, to perform his duty. He made a solemn vow, Kalina, to protect all of humanity. To protect you. And that's what he did. He sacrificed more than his life for you. He sacrificed his mind. He was taken prisoner by Nereti on purpose, let him glamour her, became her general – all to distract her." Samson chuckled. "He must have been a very good general indeed – and a good lover, if he's made Nereti fall for him."

Jaegar shook his head. "Amazing," he crowed. "Well, I don't feel so bad having Octavius for a rival. He really is that good."

Kalina turned scarlet. She didn't want to have that conversation now, in front of everybody, including her mother and brother. But she couldn't help feeling a twinge of anger. So, this was all a plan? Octavius had *chosen* to make love to Nereti? And he must have truly enjoyed her body, too, if he was able to act ecstatic so convincingly...

Jaegar put a reassuring hand on Kalina's shoulder. "I know you care for him, Kal," he said.

"And you're worried about him. But if Nereti has feelings for him now, it's the best thing for all of us. Wherever they are, he'll be safe. Nereti won't harm him."

"She healed him..." Kalina's lips were trembling. "After she almost took out his heart."

There was something utterly macho about the way Samson and Jaegar smirked at one another.

"I guess he slayed her in more ways than one," Jaegar's cocky grin was spread across his face.

"Jaegar!" Kalina was horrified at his levity.

"Sorry," Jaegar groaned. "I just can't believe Nereti would ever fall. I bet she didn't see *that* coming..."

"She guards herself well," said Samson. "But the heart is often the least protected organ of all – because it was the one she least expected would fall before another's assault. Nothing could penetrate that hardened stone – or so she thought."

Kalina decided to change the conversation. "We have to go after them. Wherever they went. Oh, Jaegar – what if she found her way into that other world? And took Octavius with her?" The thought was almost too terrible to bear. "What if we can't find him again?" Tears filled her eyes at the notion.

She could sense Jaegar's dejection, his envy. She knew what he was wondering. If she lost him, would she have such tears for him?

"Sure we will, Kal," Jaegar forced a smile onto his face. "Do you have any clue where they went?"

"I had such a strong connection with her before," said Kalina. "I could see and feel almost everything she felt. But now I can't. I feel nothing of her. It's like she figured out about onto me...and blocked me."

"Maybe it's because of me," Max said. "After all, your bond to me was stronger because of all that was happening to me. Perhaps our pull – strengthened by the diamonds – has replaced the bond between you and her."

"Mom!" Kalina hugged her mother tightly. "My bond to you *should* be stronger. But I still don't understand why we resemble *her* so closely!"

"She's the Queen of Vampires," Max said. "If

206

we are really carriers, then I guess it makes sense that we'd resemble her in some way."

"But I've lost my connection with her." Kal's voice trembled. "I don't know where they are. Now I'm afraid that they've vanished into another world – that I'll never see Octavius again...""

Chapter 18

Kalina couldn't bear the thought. Losing Octavius had been hard enough when she had thought of him as in this world, in *her* world, still attainable, if she only tapped in violently enough to the telepathic energy that connected them, if she only gave into the power that allowed her to see into his mind, and his into hers. No matter how far away he'd been, no matter how desperately he'd been placed under Nereti's spell, Kalina had always maintained a faith in their connection. She believed in him. She believed in their love. She believed that, no matter who else he loved, who else glamoured him, their telepathic bond was stronger than any other magic, any other vampire power. No longer. Now, Octavius might be in another universe, another world – a place that she could never reach or understand. Now, for the first time, Kalina began to wonder if her beloved Octavius were really well and truly lost.

But she had no time to dwell on the sadness that reared up like a savage beast in her heart. A loud roar began to echo in the cave. The sound of rocks, tumbling. Rock after rock, boulder after boulder, began to shift.

"Someone's coming." Jaegar's ears pricked up with animal precision. "We have to get out of here, now!"

Jaegar led them out of the cave. But no sooner had they escaped into the moonlit desert sands than they spied Nereti's army standing before them, led by that same, wicked-looking minion Kalina had only hours ago sent away. This one, whose name she did not know, had broad, powerful shoulders and a face marked by cruelty, with high, small eyes and a narrow, white-lipped smile.

"My Queen."

Kalina could see into the savage red eyes of all his vampire brethren. They looked angry. More than angry, she thought. They looked like they were high on bloodlust. Like they were hungry. Kalina gulped.

209

Very hungry.

"You led us on a wild goose chase, my Queen." The voice was a contemptuous voice – insubordinate. Kalina was shocked. No vampire would ever speak like that to Nereti, not unless he wanted his head forcibly torn from his body. It was an outlandishly foolish proposition, speaking like that to an Empress. Unless he didn't believe she was an Empress after all.

She put on her haughtiest face and drew herself up to her full height, hoping he did not see the fear in her eyes. "What did you say to me, fool? What are you doing back here? Did you find the diamonds or not? That's all that matters to me!"

"We have not found the diamonds," the minion's voice was low. "We travelled halfway there, and then I sent our very fastest, our swiftest scouts on ahead to scope out the terrain. And they all came back saying the very same thing. There is not a single cave, nor a single mine, in that region. But why would our Queen send us on a wild goose chase such as this, we asked? Why someone as formidable and wise as Nereti?"

"Because," Kalina said, her voice as cold as ice, "it was Nereti's will. Do you not think that someone as wise, as brave as Nereti – as you yourself say – might have a plan that the pitiful likes of you could not comprehend? Is that not more likely?"

"I may not have seen your face up close, my Queen," the vampire took a creeping step forward. "But I have gotten face to face orders from you before. And in all that time, never once have you ordered an entire army to go to a location without sending a scout out ahead first. You are notorious for using as few troops as possible, for minimizing waste. So why change the chase now?"

"These are important diamonds," Kalina snapped, hoping the vampires wouldn't hear her heart fluttering in her chest. "And it is not for you to question my demands, underling."

"Yet you send all your troops to gather something priceless? You trust even the most foolish of under-soldiers with your prize?"

Kalina began to falter. She knew that she was

211

lost. The vampires suspected something – that much certain – and there was only so much time she could gain by stalling. "I..."

But Jaegar cut in.

Before Kalina could speak, Jaegar had sprung forward, his ivory fingers tight against the vampire's long, sinewy neck.

"A-a-ah," the vampire minion gurgled as Jaegar lifted him clean off his feet. His feet kicked lamely against the empty air.

"Come any closer," Jaegar's voice was low and dangerous. "And his life will be forfeit. Mark my words."

The vampires looked nervous, exchanging glances and glares among themselves.

One rogue stepped forward, a cruel smirk upon his face. "So be it," he said. "What is one vampire among many? Kill him, and we will swarm you gladly. What we want, what we lust for, what we *ache* for – is blood. Spilled blood. We have not seen such blood for a long time, and we are itching to spill it anew."

He signaled to the other vampires to follow him.

"Looks like there's no loyalty among you rogues." Jaegar's voice did not falter, though Kalina could sense his fear. "So be it."

In a flash, Samson had thrown the ruby-encrusted stake over to Jaegar, who caught it deftly between his fingers. There was no time for the vampire minion to protest – or to scream. Jaegar had driven the ruby-encrusted stake deep within his chest, and the vampire turned to dust.

The battle had begun.

Kalina's heart was pounding. Around her, a series of images so surreal it felt like a dream. So many vampires – swarms upon swarms of opponents – coming toward them like the tidal waves of a flood. She and Jaegar, Justin and Samson, were fighting off as many as they could, but no matter how many they turned to ash, more kept on coming. Her Life's Blood was boiling; she was sweating – exhausting – overloaded – and still they kept on coming.

They fought for hours – no, Kalina thought, it

213

had been days, now. She had lost the ability to tell the time. She had lost the ability to notice sun or moon. All she could tell was that she was so hungry, that she was so tired, that she ached with an ache that was beyond any pain or understanding. She could not bear the sensation. Out of the corner of her eye, she could see Max fighting – Max, weakened through her ordeal, Max needing food, Max, as tired, maybe even more tired, than she was.

They had to survive. There was no way they could survive. There were too many of them.

They would die of exhaustion – of sun – or something. At some point, they would not be able to go on. There was Samson and Max, Jaegar and Justin, Kalina – five against so many thousands.

And then one vampire sword met the flesh of Samson's upper arm.

The sword flashed red with light and blood.

Samson screamed out loud as Kalina saw what had happened. Samson's severed arm, lying there upon the dirt. The strongest of them – laid low.

"Retreat!" Samson's voice sounded out.

"Retreat."

They scrambled back into the caves; Samson found a boulder, and with the last of his strength he shoved it against the opening to the cave.

"That'll hold them off," he gasped, barely able to get the words out through his pain. "Long enough for us...."

"We can't go on!" Kalina said. "We need to find a way out."

"Not all of us," Jaegar's face was grim. "They're full of blood lust and anger. Now that they've injured one of us, their resolve has been renewed. They're confused, lost, desperate. Their real queen and general are nowhere to be found. If we don't distract them here, who knows what they'll do? Maurade, ravage, go into nearby towns and villages, kill everyone they see..."

Max was coughing up blood. Her thin frame was shaking.

"Look at her!" Kalina cried. "She can't go on. She hasn't eaten for two days. I know she has Carrier blood in her, but she's a human. She needs

215

food." Her stomach growled with what she had not dared to say. *So do I.*

"We need to get you two out of here." Jaegar's eyes were dark and grim. "You need to run. The rest of us will hold them off."

Kalina's stomach dropped as she realized what he meant.

"We can't go at once or they'll follow. We three will fight. You two need to fly...you need food. You need to get us help.

"You can't hold them off..." Kalina's voice faltered. "Not with just three of you. Two – because Samson's lost a hand..."

Jaegar pulled Kalina so close that she could smell the heat of him. He kissed her violently, passionately, a kiss that sent her reeling with desire and with fear. The kind of kiss you only give when you know you're saying goodbye.

"I love you, Kal. And with my last breath I will defend you, and your kind. You and Max cannot die yet. It's not your time. You need be strong, Kalina..."

"No!" She couldn't be strong without him.

"You need to lead other carriers, rebuild the vampire consortium against these kinds of vampire, against all evil, you need to live on. I'll fight them off. I'm the strongest one left. I can take on these peons..." He grinned, and he was almost like his old self again. "As if they're nothing. Please, Kal. Let me do this. Let me give you your life. And if I can't live to be with you, if I can't live long enough to see you live your life, then at least let me go out this way. In a way befitting of my love for you."

She could not hold back her sobs. "Jaegar, no, please! You can't mean this. It's not goodbye – it's *not.*"

But in her heart, she knew it was. As Max pried her out of Jaegar's arms, she knew that this goodbye would be forever.

Max's arms were around her, Max was pulling her, Max was flying with her, through the air, and Jaegar was getting smaller and smaller.

She could hear Jaegar's voice echoing to her on the wind.

"This is the day all the good vampires, all the

217

humans who know our story, will remember. The day that we, the last remaining members of the Consortium, defended to the death all that is good, all that is pure. All that is life."

She could hear the boulder being rolled away.

"Charge!"

Chapter 19

They were flying as fast as they could. Kalina's adrenaline was pumping through her; her blood was boiling within her veins. Her arms were around her mother's waist, barely keeping her up; she could feel how exhausted Max was, after her injury; how much she needed to eat. She was numb, utterly numb. Jaegar might be dying in the battle below, but she couldn't feel it. She'd gone through so much in the past few hours that she was unable to feel anything at all. Her pain was a dull, white force, like a fog, that obscured her from the reality of what was happening. All she could focus on was the need to get back to town, back to the hotel, to get something to eat.

"There are lots of street vendors nearby," Max said. "I'll get us some food, okay. You go to the hotel. You need to recharge."

Blood Curse (Pulse #8)

It was so strange, Kalina thought, to be in such a crowded place, such a crowded, *normal* place, when a battle was raging on a few minutes' flight away. As she sat on the hotel bed, the silks so soft beneath her skin, she could almost believe that she was a normal girl, a normal human being. That her life was anything other than what it was.

In the corner was Jaegar's bag, slumped over a chair. She noticed it with a pang. How could it be that Jaegar was risking his life miles away – and she wasn't there to see it? She walked over to the bag and brushed it lightly with her fingers, trying to inhale the scent of him, trying to breathe in one last breath of his sweat, his musk, the intoxicating aroma of his body.

She saw it glittering in the bag. At first, she was not sure what it was. She reached out her hand and picked it up: a glimmering ring. An enormous diamond, in an old wooden box that had fallen open, a dark wood so deep it was nearly black. At first, she thought, it looked like --- could it be? A diamond ring...

220

She swallowed down her tears. Had Jaegar been about to propose? Surely not. He knew about her feelings for Octavius; he knew she was in no position to make her final choice about the man, the one man, she was destined to forever love.

And then the diamond changed color. It grew red, then orange, then yellow – a whole rainbow swirl.

Kalina blinked through her tears and then the colors were gone. The diamond was just as it had been before.

The door opened behind her.

"Mom," she turned to see Max, empty-handed. "Where's the food?"

"What are you looking at?" Max motioned to the ring.

"I..." Kalina swallowed. "I don't know. I don't know what it is. It was Jaegar's. But why would he carry it around, all this time, and not give it to me?"

Max began to frown. "Give it to me." She reached for it so violently that Kalina instinctively stepped back. "Now."

"Mom, what is it?"

This voice, high and cold, wasn't like her mother. Those eyes, with such hate and cruelty in them, were not the eyes she knew and loved.

"All this time – right under my nose...all this time." She reached for it again; again Kalina pulled it away.

"Mom, calm down..." But Kalina had a sneaking suspicion it wasn't her mother that clutched for the ring.

"Come, now, girl. Don't you know you must always obey your mother..."

"Why?"

"Because..." Max's voice had dropped lower; it was huskier, more full of rage. "I say so." Her body was moving; her shape was shifting; before Kalina knew it, it was Nereti that stood before her, a cruel glower upon her face.

"Nereti?" Kalina's heart dropped into the pit of her stomach as horror overtook her. "But...where's Max? What have you done with her?"

"She is..." Nereti looked almost confused. "She

is...where I was." For a moment it seemed as if Nereti herself were unsure of what was going on. "On her way to a place you will never reach."

"Your home?"

Nereti's smile was thin. "Yes. I must confess, I did not expect to change places with her. Such a thing is unheard of in vampire lore. And it was not by my own art that I find myself here, or her there. But I am so glad it has occurred. For it means I can kill you, as I always meant to do. I felt something, some presence, lurking at the back of my mind. I thought it was you, at first. An insolent fool trying to read my thoughts. But now I know the truth. It is her that is the true link to me, not you. The older one. When she was able to withstand so much of the crystal, that great gem of the Old Place, that was when I knew. I understand it all, now..."

"Well, I don't." Kalina's voice was tight with fear.

"A Life's Blood Carrier who shares your blood. That is the combination we have all been seeking. The crystals and your blood – combined into a single potent force. That is what I need. That is what I seek. The very substance of my body's make-up, which originates and has its life in the land of magic, beyond the crystal river. The land of the Fey. Not this forsaken land of filthy mortality."

"I don't understand."

"They call me 'vampire' now. Those who are suspicious of me. Those who know nothing. They call me the name of those little bats that hide in caves from fear. But I have another name, a truer name. Just as Columbus called 'Indians' those natives on a shore of which he knew nothing, so too do they call me by that which makes it easier for them to understand." Nereti drew herself up to her full, imperious height. "No, I am a creature of the Fey...the 'Dark' Fey, now and forever. That is my pride. That is my heritage. That is the blood of which I am most proud. Our race, that must destroy yours, which means nothing."

"Well, if you like the Crystal River so much, maybe you should go back there." Kalina tried to sound braver than she felt.

224

"Not without magic, my girl. But now you have the magic I seek. And if I have to kill you to get home, that would be an added bonus."

"So if we're so non-magical here, how come we have all the magic, huh? Maybe you're not giving our humans enough credit."

"Enough talk!" cried Nereti. "I am weary of your prattle. I wish to kill you now."

But before she could act, the door flung open.

Max was standing in the doorway – the real Max – and with her the most handsome man Kalina had ever seen. The man who made her heart beat so fast she thought it would burst. Octavius.

"Kal!" Max cried. "I don't know what happened! One second I was in line for food, and the next I was suddenly...with Octavius. As if we..."

"Traded places," Nereti spun around to face Max.

"Kal..." Octavius' voice was so dreamy Kalina could have swooned. "I'm back – and ready to wreak revenge on my old tormentor..."

"Get away from her," Max's voice was shaking.

"Kal...come to me. Don't believe a word she says about her intentions. She's lying, through and through. I heard her thoughts. I heard everything. She doesn't just want to go home. If she returns to where she came from – she'll slaughter and destroy their world the way she's tried to do in ours. We can't banish her. We can only kill her. We have to stop her."

Nereti's laugh was sickening. "Not if I can help it," she cackled.

At once she was at Max's side. "Pretty," she crowed, motioning toward the diamond ring on Max's finger. In an instant she had whipped out a sharp silver blade and severed the finger, the ring still gleaming.

Max yelped in pain but it was too late. Nereti was already by the window.

"Pity..." Nereti's eyes were smoldering on Octavius. "We could have had so much fun together. I should have known the milk of human kindness would dull your sensual instincts."

And with that, she was gone in the blink of an

eye.

Kalina couldn't care. Octavius was here; that was what mattered. She ran into Octavius' arms, overjoyed to have his lips press hers once more. Her love for him came rushing in like a flood.

"I missed you so much" she cried.

"You too, my dear one," Octavius whispered.

"I know why you did it. Like a general. For the cause."

"But my heart was always with you," he stroked her hair.

"I know," she kissed him harder. "I know that now."

"Come on." Max's voice interrupted them. Kalina looked on in wonder – her mother's finger had already grown back. Was it because of the diamonds or rather, the crystals she ingested? "Let's eat and then head back to the battle. We've wasted enough time. We have to go help the others."

"Yes," Kalina said.

"Here," Max handed her a box of food. "Gulp down and drink some water. Octavius and I will head on out now, and you can follow after. Bring more rubies." She indicated the bag and began to fill her breast pockets with rubies.

"A shield!" Kalina said. "You're making a shield with those rubies."

"Exactly. We can't be too safe. This battle will be our most dangerous yet. Now gulp down that food – and let's go."

******

The battle was underway. By the time Kalina had arrived at the cave complex she had left behind not too long ago, she saw at once that the numbers of Nereti's minions had been diminished. There were only half as many as there had been. And they were still fighting – a sure sign that at least some of those she loved were still alive. But which ones? She couldn't say. She squinted to make them out.

At last she spotted Samson, fighting with his one good arm with all of his strength, Octavius and Max already at his side. But there was no sign of Justin or Jaegar anywhere.

228

Octavius had the advantage. Many of the fighters still recognized him as loyal to Nereti, which gave him the element of surprise, and he was able to slaughter twenty at a single flash of his sword before they realized he had sided with Kalina now. But there were still many minions left to conquer, and only a few of them left.

At last they were able to push the intruders back to the mouth of the cave, buying them some more time to recuperate. Samson lined the entrance to the cave with rubies, knowing it would repel the vampires.

And then Kalina saw it. She cried aloud with horror. Justin's body lying down on the ground, his body twisted in an unnatural position. She couldn't think. Her mind went blank. Here was her brother, her beloved brother, lying in a pool of blood.

She turned him over, gasping with terror. "Justin, no, no please! Justin, you can't be...I can't lose you a second time." She was screaming; she was hysterical. Her own brother, the brother she loved so deeply – she knew she would not be able to bear

229

losing him.

"That won't help, Kal." Octavius' voice was soft and low alongside her.

"Then..."

Octavius' smile was wry. "He's a vampire, Kal. And vampires...they turn to ash when they die."

How could she have been so stupid? Even after all this time, she couldn't get used to thinking of Justin as a vampire.

"He's alive?" She could have danced in happiness.

Justin opened his eyes and groaned. "Can't a guy get a break to rest here?" Good old Justin, Kalina thought. Keeping his good humor in spite of everything. "All this screaming and crying is really cutting into my beauty sleep."

"Justin!" Kalina hugged him so tight he bolted upright. "You're alive! I mean – you're here!"

"Of course?" Justin beamed up at her. "I wouldn't leave my baby sister to fight alone, now would I? We may not be related by blood, but you're still my baby sister, and I still love you. I'm your big bro. And I'm here to stay."

"And Jaegar?"

Justin looked up in confusion. "He's not here?" He wiped the blood off his face. "I could have sworn..." He looked around. "The vampire that left this mess on me – Jaegar was rushing at him. That's the last thing I remember. He saved my skin, Jaegar did. Staked at least one vamp. Then..."

Kalina's face fell. Surely Jaegar had to be somewhere. He had to be alive! He couldn't be...that was too terrible to think about.

They all looked around, among the piles of ash, with fear and trepidation, hoping against hope they wouldn't find any sign of...

"Oh, no." Octavius' voice was full of pain.

"What is it?"

Octavius was holding a Life's Blood ring. Engraved in the band were those letters she knew so well. JG. Jaegar Greystone. He would never leave it anywhere. He would never give it up. Unless...

Unless he were a pile of ash like the others.

"No!" Kalina began to cry out. "No!" She was

sobbing, wailing, screaming; she could not bear the pain. Her beloved, her dear one, her Jaegar.

Gone. All gone.

Chapter 20

When Kalina woke up, it took her a while to realize where she was. She wasn't in a cave, nor in an African hotel room. She was in her own room, in her own bed, in Rutherford. What was this – some sort of dream? Had she died, out there, in the caves? But the light felt real, streaming as it did through the window-panes; the sun on her face felt real.

"How long have I been sleeping?" Her voice sounded like it was coming from a million miles away. "What the..."

Octavius' lips were cool on her forehead. "You've been out for a week, my love."

Grief. Waves of grief. So much grief she could not bear it. All coming over her, all at once. The memory of her loss, savage and anew. She could not stand it. She could not even weep.

"She's up?"

Jaegar! For a moment she was sure – so sure – it was his voice. It had all been a dream, that was it. A terrible nightmare. He was alive; he was safe; he was...

"Stuart?"

The same voice as his brother. The same face. But such a different manner. Elegant and refined where Jaegar was raffish and laid-back. Normally the sight of Stuart would fill her with relief. But now it only brought back the pain. He was half a pair. And the other half was dead.

"Kal!" Stuart's arms were tight around her. The last time he'd held her, there had been a tension – unbearable, devastating, the force of his desire. But this time he was looking at her, holding her differently. As a brother. As a friend.

"I'm so sorry, Kal," Stuart whispered.

"No, I'm sorry..." Kalina's voice was hoarse. "He's your brother. I know you must be missing him more than anyone."

"I know," Stuart said softly. "I know how much we fought. But deep down we loved each other. Deep

234

down, he was my brother. The second brother I've lost." His voice wavered and he cleared his throat. "But, Kal, he died doing what he loved best. And none of us can cheat death forever. Most of us don't even want to. All I know is – I hope to see him again in the afterlife." He stroked her hair. "I know how much he loved you, Kalina. So very desperately. He would want you to live on, to be happy."

"That's right." A sweet, melodic female voice echoed through the room. Kalina looked up with joy to see her best friend Maeve in the doorway. "Kal, we're so happy to have you back home."

She was different from how Kalina had last seen her. More beautiful. Happier. There was the glow of love upon her face.

"There's so much we have to tell you." Maeve took Stuart's hand.

And then Kalina understood.

She could have burst out laughing. What a perfect pairing! She should have seen it coming from day one. Sweet, kind Maeve and honorable, upright Stuart – the ideal couple. They were made for each

235

other. And though deep down she felt a twinge of nostalgia for what had passed between them, the idea that Stuart would end up like this, with a woman who was right for him at last, who truly loved him with an undivided heart, gave her great joy.

"You two?"

"Fighting off vampires together sure brings you closer, huh?" Maeve' smile was sparkling.

"I know how that feels," said Justin, putting a gentle hand on Kalina's shoulder. "We're closer as a family than ever."

Max came over to Kalina. "You will get through this, Kalina. I know how hard it is, losing someone you love. I have done it more times than I can count. But I promise, every day gets easier."

Kalina could not imagine how it could get easier. How would she ever be able to say goodbye to Jaegar?

"You passed out for a long time," said Octavius. "In that time, we did what we could to honor Jaegar's memory. There is an urn in the Greystone family mausoleum – that testifies to his

236

honor in battle."

Max kissed Kalina's forehead lightly. "Maybe you might find it helpful to say goodbye, too?"

But she couldn't do it. Kalina spent hours in front of the crypt, in front of the photograph of Jaegar surrounded by lilies and roses, and found that she did not have the words.

At last, as the sunset spread across the sky and cast its rosy shadow on the grass, she tried to reach out to him, telepathically; one last, desperate attempt at love.

How could you do this? How could you be so stupid? You gave your life – but at what cost? I can't go on without you. I can't be the Carrier without you. I know you wanted to be the hero, but I wish you'd stayed with me instead. I know it's wrong but I do. You died too soon, Jaegar. You died before I could tell you everything. Before I could tell you how much I loved you, how strongly I really felt about you, about us. I can't handle my love for you. It's too strong. When I saw that ring in your bag, I thought it was an engagement ring. And all I could think was...I would have said yes, Jaegar. I would have said yes to you.

She heard a rustling in the bushes and looked up. For a moment she had hope that her words had summoned him. But there was no one there. No Jaegar by her side.

Alone she walked through the fields, toward the Greystone mansion. She wanted Max, her mother. She wanted Justin. She wanted to mourn in the arms of her family.

But when she entered the house, it was Octavius she saw.

Kalina could not hold back her tears. She ran to him. She sobbed, at last, letting him feel all her pain, all her anguish, all her utter exhaustion at all that she had lost.

Jaegar was gone. Octavius was here.

There was nothing standing in their way.

She only wanted to forget her pain.

"Please," she whispered. She wrapped her arms around him. She took his face in her hands. She kissed him violently. "Please, make me forget."

She could see the desire in his eyes. She

wanted him to unleash it at last.

They kissed with hungrier and hungrier motions; soon, they had stripped down to their underwear; soon, they were lying on the rug in front of the fireplace, his chest against hers. Oh, how she wanted him like this! How she wanted to feel him inside her in reality, and not in her imagination!

"Please," she said again.

"Are you sure? Do you want this?"

"I know I do."

"You know the consequences?" It was his General voice – authoritative and firm.

"I do."

"And even knowing them?"

"I'm more sure than about anything in my life."

"And do you love me – as I do you?" Octavius' voice wavered there.

"I have always loved you."

"And Jaegar?" His tone turned dark.

"He's gone!" She couldn't bear to think of it.

"And you love him still..." Octavius' voice was

hollow.

"I loved him, I don't deny it," Kalina said. "But when I saw you and Nereti together – the jealousy, the pain I experienced, it made me worried about the love you might have for me. I love you, Octavius – but could I not ask you, whether you love me completely, too? You enjoyed being with her a lot..."

"It was entirely one-sided," Octavius said. "I thought only of you when I was with her. But with you and Jaegar – it was more than that. You truly loved him. It should have been him."

"Don't say that!" She wanted to forget Jaegar, forget her pain. "I could make you human, Octavius. I could end your suffering."

Octavius gently shook his head and touched his fingertips to the sides of Kalina's face. "I'm sorry, Kal. I heard you at the grave. I didn't mean to listen to your thoughts. I came to look for you – I heard everything, telepathically. And I'm so afraid, if we do this, and if I'm not the one, it will turn me into a cruel beast like Mal."

"You are the one!"

"I want to be *sure* Kalina. Sure that this isn't just a rebound for you. I will wait for you." He kissed her deeply. "As long as I have to. Forever, if I have to."

She reached up and touched his lips.

"Will you give me some time?"

Soon, she would know herself. Soon, she would move on. Soon, she would be able to love him, completely. But forgetting Jaegar wouldn't be that easy.

A sparkle caught Kalina's eye. She looked down and gasped. Octavius was holding out the ring.

"I found this, with Jaegar's....with the ash." he said. "I took it into my laboratory to do some research. And Kalina, there's something you should know..."

Epilogue

Gliding through the air. Slicing through the sky. Faster than a thousand horses, swifter than the swiftest chariot. Nereti was whipping through the sky. She could feel her pursuer. She could feel the breeze on her skin as she grew near. This strange man who was able to hurt her. Octavius? It couldn't be – she'd left him behind. It had to be someone else.

This vampire was as swift as she was. But how could it be? Nobody was as swift as Nereti, the great Empress. The Queen. The Dark Fey.

Once, she had been of another kind. She had been a pixie, then, a Dark Fey, and the most powerful pixie in Feyland. But her power had not been strong enough. She had wanted more. Then she had discovered that human blood – the blood of mortals beyond the Crystal River – could add to her power. The iron in human blood would turn the green blood of the pixies a dark red, giving them new stamina. They would be beautiful, like the Winter or the Summer Fey. For beauty was power, wasn't it? Wasn't it? That's what she'd always thought. That's what she'd always believed. That was why the Fey utilize glamouring as a strong magic...to provide the illusion of beauty or power.

She had sent a pixie scout beyond the crystal river, so many centuries ago, to abduct a human virgin girl, ripe for the sacrifice. A girl with caramel skin and dark ravens'-wing hair, with chocolate eyes and full, full lips. A girl desired by all the men in the village. But no mortal man could have her for his bride. Death would claim her.

Nereti had not known about the curse. She had not known that the peasant who loved the young woman most of all would go to a local alchemist, to beg him to put a spell on his beloved: that only her true love would be able to have her, while all who loved her for her body would be made monstrous in her eyes. She would not have bit into the girl's neck if she had known. She would not have been such a fool.

The girl had fought her off, of course. The girl, named for the beauty of the jade stone, was as hard as her namesake. She had not given up easily. But in the end she had succumbed, with the words that haunted Nereti now.

"You may have my blood, demon, but you will never have my strength. You are a demon, and no human blood will turn you human. You will forever live in darkness. May you never walk in human lands with ease again. You will not feel the light of the sun nor the light of love. My beloved swore he would protect me with this curse; may his protection extend now to all of my kind. Since you have taken my blood to the point of death, you will have his curse. But never will you have the enchantment of love. Only love can break the curse."

What foolishness, Nereti had thought, sucking the blood greedily as the girl had died.

She had gone to the mirror. She had rejoiced in her new self: her new skin, her new hair, her new chocolate eyes. She now had the mortal girl's beauty.

Then she had opened her mouth. Then she had seen the fangs. The fangs had sliced into her lips, making her bleed red.

Then she had felt the hunger. The need. The insatiable appetite that had become a curse. That sent her into human lands, desperate for food, desperate to cross the Crystal River into the land whose heat and light she could no longer withstand.

She had led raiding parties, at first. Gone back and forth. Stolen more virgin girls known for their beauty and youth. Figured their sacrifice was worth it, if it meant more power.

Then the wolves had gotten to her. Now ordinary wolves, but the ones filled with fey magic, from Feyland...a special breed known as the Wolf Fey...more shifters than werewolves, shifting to human form and to beast, larger than any wolves known in the Crystal Realms. Those blasted werewolves, meddling where they weren't wanted. Prattling on about the dignity of human life. They'd banished her, once and for all, from the Crystal River and from the Feyland that was her home.

She would get back there one day. There, she would rule. That was her plan, all along. It was she that had compelled that doctor from China to create the Carriers – posing as a young apprentice. She had put the idea into his head. A being capable of vampire power without vampire curses. A new breed of vampire for her army. How could she have known that they would turn to the side of the humans, of their protectors?

Still she had hope. It was why she could not bring herself to kill Kalina, as often as she'd had the chance. These Carriers were the secret to restoring her old self, the pixie self, the self without these terrible cravings...

The self Octavius might have loved.

No, she did not love. She was a Queen, above all that. Then why did she feel this pain? Why did she miss him so badly?

She would think no more of it.

She was close to the Crystal River, now, with the ring in hand, the ring that would allow her to cross up....the river was shining before her.

"Hold it." A cocky male voice. The voice of a mere youth.

"What do you want, minion?" she snarled. "How were you able to follow me to this place?'

"It's Jaegar to you, Your Highness." The Pursuer. He was the one chasing her through the air just now. His words were dripping with sarcasm. "Maybe this will explain it." He flashed her a ring of his own... "Looks like diamonds are a boy's best friend, huh? Especially magic diamonds like these. Made with crystals from the Crystal River, right? I did my research."

"How did you get that?"

"Let's just say I'm good with my hands?" Jaegar said. "And that's nothing compared to what these hands are going to do to you. You hurt and almost killed everyone I love. Now, it's time for my revenge. So you're not going to cross, my dear. Not if I can help it. It's time for you to pay for what you've done."

Blood Curse (Pulse #8)

A growl almost inhuman, came from a space on the other side of the icy river. No mortal eyes can see beyond the river to see the enormous brown wolf, one that had shifted, crouching there, ready to pounce. A werewolf. A guardian. Werewolves and vampires had always been at odds with each other. No, even at war with each other. This one was also fey. One of the wolf fey from Feyland. And he was determined to stop her from passing through from the mortal world to the land of the fey.

"Who are you to stop me, wolf!" Nereti sneered.

"The Prince," the wolf shifted into a very handsome tall and muscular young man with chestnut hair and hazel eyes. He appeared to be in his early 20s, as a human. Nereti had seen and ruled many mortal and vampire men before, but this wolf fey was quite extraordinary. His broad shoulders and confident stature reminded her of Octavius, yet his kind eyes brought Stuart Greystone to mind. As he

248

stepped forward past the border of the Ring of Ice protecting the portal between Feyland and the Land Beyond the Crystal River, his shape became more solid and his voice boomed loud enough to announce his entrance. "I am Logan, the Wolf Fey Prince, and guardian of these borders."

Jaegar's blue eyes nearly bulged out of his sockets. "Damn, what do they feed you over there, genetically-enhanced dog food?"

Logan took one look at Jaegar and smirked. "More like ground minotaurs and an occasional vampire or dark fey, as we call you guys, over there."

"I thought werewolves were fictional," Jaegar said, scratching his head. "Of all the years I've been a vampire I've never encountered one...until now."

Logan laughed. "My ancestors did an awesome job spinning that tale and making us into some kind of legend out here. The stories began long ago when one of our wolf fey began transforming into a wolf and then was seen walking upright like a man, while still in transformation." Logan peered down at Jaegar. "I travel back and forth all the time between Feyland and The Crystal Realms, but I haven't seen you before."

"That's because I've never been this close to that portal there, what is it? A wall of ice?"

Nereti was peering at the wall, where icicles formed a circular ring. "I see the Winter Lands there. Feyland, the origin of magic, the birthplace of mine."

Logan stepped forward to block Nereti from moving closer to the ring of ice. He raised his sword that glinted wickedly from the small ray of light from the moon. "You, Dark Fey, and enemy to humans and fey alike, will have to go through me to get back to Feyland. I know your plans...you are seeking ultimate power of both Feyland and the Crystal Realms. I can't let you claim that."

Jaegar stepped forth too, facing Nereti and crossing his arms over his chest. "Seems like I'm in agreement with the Wolf. I can't let you do that, too, Witchy Poo. Trying to take over the human world is bad enough, but now that place of his, what do you call it? It appears a bit frosty there..."

"Feyland," Logan said.

"Feyland, thank you," Jaegar said to Logan before turning to face Neriti. "You do just a little too much of taking. I know because I have always taken what I wanted, too, but no, not like you. You make me look like a generous donor. All that greed you have...well, it's time to start giving back."

Logan stared hard at Neriti as though he was able to see right through her. "No, it can't be," he said. "I think I remembered being told about you from fey history...the first fey to be cast out of Feyland...Pixie King Delano's first wife who

251

committed the most heinous crime that threatens the boundaries between all that is supernatural and human. With all the murders that you committed of fey and humans alike in order to sustain your beauty and power, you created the curse which now this young vampire bears for eternity. Not only were you a Pixie Queen who put the idea into Delano's head to start a war between the Summer and Winter Kingdom, but you opened the portals between Feyland and the Dark Worlds to let the witches into Feyland where they practice their sith ways of deceiving the public with their lies, getting families and authorities to trust them and then slaughtering, sacrificing fey children and virgins to you. So evil are you and your witches that you sacrificed your own children, offering their souls up to demons in order for you to keep your wealth and position."

"Holy Mother..." Jaegar let out a big breath. "I had no idea you were that evil...I mean, you take the cake in the holy grail of evil, Neriti."

Logan looked over at Jaegar. "So you see, there is no way in hell this woman will ever get back into Feyland or any of the Frost Worlds, or as you would like to call it, the supernatural world...if I can help it."

Nereti stood up straighter, her eyes glittering with mirth and arrogance. "Too late, Wolf Prince. The thing about being a fey and a vampire? We can glamour and compel. We are faster than fey. And as a vampire, we can transport ourselves a great distance in a flash."

Logan looked over at the shattered wall of ice and saw a figure, dressed like Nereti running across the frozen waters of the Crystal River. He glanced back at Nereti, and in a flash, she was gone.

He looked accusingly at Jaegar, who looked just as dumbfounded as he did.

"I saw as much as you did," Jaegar said. "And believe me, that came out of nowhere." He groaned as Logan shook his head and gave a great big wolf howl, alerting the Wolf Fey from the other side of the wall in Feyland about Neriti and got ready to jump through the wall to give chase to the running figure.

Jaegar groaned. "I am getting too old for this, chasing rogue vampires around. Now Neriti's escaped...how am I supposed to tell Kal and the gang back home I've let the biggest evil that ever walked the Earth out of my sight?"

Logan grabbed Jaegar's wrist and pulled him with him almost through the portal when Jaegar tried to fight him off. "Let me go now, Wolf!" Jaegar said.

"No, I have to keep an eye on you, too," Logan said. "Plus you know something about her that we can find useful."

"I say, let me go!" Jaegar struggled against the strong grip the Wolf Prince had on him. "If you don't," Jaegar said after a few more attempts to free himself, "then this invisible being holding only my other wrist will get through and..."

Logan sliced through the air between Jaegar's other wrist and what appeared to be nothing, and heard a woman's cry in pain. "Beast!" she spat, before materializing into Neriti. "Looks like I have to fight against you two before I can get anywhere..."

Jaegar and Logan looked at each other and turned their heads back to nod at Neriti. "Yup!"

*****

Kalina, Jaegar, Octavius, and the PULSE Vampire Family story continues in Book 9: Blood Ring.

Sparklesoup.com

THE PULSE VAMPIRE BOOK SERIES - Now Complete and Available!

PULSE
Life's Blood
Blood Burn
Blue Blood
The PULSE Papers - Novella
Blood Bond
Blood Legacy

Blood Curse (Pulse #8)

Blood Rights
Blood Curse
Blood Ring
Ring of Ice

Brotherhood of Blood

Want More Edgy books like *PULSE*?

visit

Sparklesoup.com

Where you will find edgy books for teens and young adults that would make your heart pound, your skin crawl, and leave you wanting more...

Feed Your Reading Addiction

Blood Curse (Pulse #8)

Sign up for news, book giveaways, author signings, ARC giveaways, promotions, specials, contests, job announcements, events, and more!

!